RESCUING EMERY

BROTHERHOOD PROTECTORS WORLD

BARB HAN

Twisted Page Press LLC

BROTHERHOOD PROTECTORS

ORIGINAL SERIES BY ELLE JAMES

Brotherhood Protectors Series

To Elle James for letting me write in your world and introducing me to your awesome readers—a huge thank you. You already know how much I love you.
To Ali Williams for another outstanding editing job. You make me a better writer.
To Tori, proofreader extraordinaire. You are the best and I love working with you.

CHAPTER 1

"Going up tomorrow?"

Kathrine Kilbourne seemed hellbent on convincing Ash Cage that strapping wood to his feet and rocketing down the side of a mountain was a good idea.

"I didn't leave anything up there," he answered with a wink. The air was brisk. The days short. Ash's first February in a wintery state had him questioning his life choices. He might hate the cold with a passion, but it was a helluva lot better than the desert. And as much as he loved his home state of Texas, he was nowhere near ready to face it again.

"You have time to come in for a bite?"

Kat, as she'd asked Ash to call her, glanced toward the sky and the snowflakes coming down, that were already decreasing visibility. With business down for the seventy-year-old widow, despite favorable snow conditions, the invites for food had become a regular occurrence. Not that Ash was complaining.

"I can spare a few minutes before I should probably head home." He rented a small cabin a mile up the road. Realtors would call the place *rustic*. It was a two-room cabin with a stove for heat and original wood floors, though Ash didn't mind the tight quarters; it was all the space he and his dog, Seven, needed.

"I've got coffee. Strong and hot. Just like you like it. And a biscuit for my favorite four-legged friend." Today's work was ending early thanks to a white-out warning. This blizzard was supposed to be the big one. The kind of snow-dump that caused skiers and snowboarders to fly hundreds of miles for the chance to carve the mountain in fresh powder.

"Seven would eat store bought treats if he was hungry enough."

"He deserves better than that." Kat wagged her finger. "A dog that saved as many lives as him should have the very best."

Ash didn't disagree. "Yes, ma'am."

Kat made a show of looking over her shoulder. "Is *she* standing right behind me?"

"Who?"

"My mother-in-law. Because I know you're not using that formal word with me."

He apologized, and she chuckled. Calling Mrs. Kilbourne by her first name would take some getting used to. Ash's deep-seated southern upbringing caused him to slip on occasion, calling her the 'M' word as she'd so often teased when he referred to her as *ma'am*.

Old habits died hard. When he'd settled in Hero's Junction last summer he'd been concerned about Kat. On the surface, she was an aging woman living alone. He'd worried a transient might take advantage of the situation. After getting to know her, Ash feared for the man or woman crazy enough to take the feisty widow on. Not only did she sleep with an axe and a shotgun next to her bed, she knew how to use both.

"Door will be unlocked when you're ready."

"Yes, ma—...*Kat.*"

"See there. That wasn't so bad, was it?" She smiled, turned and disappeared into the house looking satisfied. In addition to daily yoga classes, the woman chopped her own wood and still found time to bake muffins so good they could make a grown man cry. She came alive playing hostess to guests of her motel, a roadside haunt for snowboarders and skiers by the name of Snowed Inn, and kept up with fourteen rooms, making them clean and comfortable for travelers.

Her downfall? By her own admission, she couldn't wield a wrench or a screwdriver if her life depended on it. Those, she'd said, she was allergic to.

That's where Ash's skills came in handy. He'd shown up with nothing more than a military-issue duffel and desire for work. She'd seen to the rest.

"Seven," Ash called. His dog had been a bomb detector for the Delta Force Unit until his age dictated retirement. He'd been the best at his job. All total, he'd led about four hundred patrols and no solider was ever injured when Seven was walking for them.

Caring for Seven had given Ash a renewed sense of purpose after he'd been medically boarded out of the military.

Ash whistled. The German shepherd came barreling around the corner. Ears forward, nose down, Seven must've finished checking the property —a routine he performed on every job site and back at home.

"Good, boy." Ash intentionally spoke English instead of German. He didn't want any confusion for Seven about his new life.

Unhooking his tool belt, he tossed it inside the passenger seat of his 1972 pickup, Tabasco, named for its spicy red paint job. Pain shot through his right hand. It twitched. Damn IED. He cursed the nerve damage that made using his dominant hand a challenge.

Ash got by fine with his disability pay and by doing odd jobs on the mountain and around town. Kat's place was for diehard skiers and snowboarders who didn't have the budget to stay slope side; receiving none today wasn't a good sign her business was about to pick up.

Kat appeared at the doorway. Spunky was too small a word to describe her. "Better come inside while the muffins are hot and before the storm gets any closer." She clucked her tongue toward the gray clouds. "This one's shaping up to be a real doozy."

"They say it'll be the worst so far this winter." Ash hated the snow. The isolation and temporary nature of living within a stone's throw of a ski resort was the perk that had him settling in unfamiliar Hero's Junction instead of returning to his hometown in Texas a decorated war hero. Hero? Not him. Four of his best friends had died on the day Ash had carried a local woman for twenty-six hours to reach her village. Meanwhile, his friends paid the ultimate price for their service. They were the heroes.

The best part of living in Colorado was the fact folks seemed to know when to pry and when to leave a man alone. People talked, probably wondered, but they didn't ask him questions about his past or why he'd turned up in town and that suited him fine.

Besides, folks moved to Colorado as much for the solitude as for the views. For Ash, the air was crisp and clean here and nothing like the thick, sweltering scent of death like in Afghanistan.

"Let's go, boy." Seven took his usual spot in front of Ash, leading the way inside the house. Nose to the floor, he began his methodical check. Every room had to be cleared before Seven could settle down.

The first couple of months Seven had come to live with Ash had been the most difficult. The adjustment for dog and owner had taken a minute to get used to and then there was the issue of both being out of work for the first time.

Seven had been restless. He'd had more energy than Ash knew what to do with. The rub in the situation was that Ash felt the same. He understood his new companion a little too well because he found himself in the same predicament. Didn't change the fact Ash didn't know what to do to solve the problem but he'd heard the saying acknowledging it was step one.

And then one day it finally clicked. They needed a routine. Ash was already used to five a.m. wake up. It was filling their waking hours that created the challenge. Seven had served his country well and deserved the best life possible in retirement, so, Ash had borrowed Mrs. Kilbourne's computer to research transitioning military K-9s.

Each morning, Seven needed to search every room before walking the perimeter to check for non-existent explosives. Ash got used to waiting for Seven to search the interior and exterior of the cabin before anything else could happen. Like clockwork at first light, his new companion made the rounds. Same was true when he visited Mrs. Kilbourne and every other home or business.

First, Seven had to go nose-to-ground, quietly sniffing each room until he knew it was safe. Then, Ash could discuss the job.

Patience brought out the best in Seven. Quirks and all, he was the best damn dog Ash had ever known.

Of course, Seven's oddities proved tricky for Ash's profession, but folks cared for each other in Hero's Junction. Word had quickly spread, and people welcomed Seven into their homes, accepting him and his limitations.

Ash had to keep vigilant watch if there was a child around. Patrol dogs were known to bite and that didn't make for a good pet. It was the reason Seven's handler hadn't been able to keep him. Ron Henry had a young family in Fort Bragg, North Carolina and three additional years of service ahead of him. He couldn't risk Seven at home with his wife and a two-year-old while deployed thousands of miles away in the dessert. It took special training to handle a patrol dog.

"Here you go." Kat set a cup of coffee and a plate with two blueberry muffins on the table, motioning for Ash to take a seat.

She joined him at the table, waiting patiently for Seven to finish his routine so she could give him a biscuit.

Her cell vibrated on the counter. She reached for it, checked the screen and put it to her ear in a heartbeat. "What can I do for you, Juan?"

Ash finished the last bite of muffin and emptied his coffee cup. He set the mug on the table. His exit just presented itself. Sheriff Juan Morales was most likely checking on Kat to make sure she had everything she needed ahead of the storm.

Ash moved next to the door as she pointed to a bag of fresh muffins meant for him to take home. She was too good to him.

"Oh. Is that right? That's troublesome." She stopped him in his tracks with the concerned glance she shot, eyebrows pinched together.

"Yes, he's right here." She held out the phone. "Sheriff wants to talk to you."

"Me?" Ash took the offering. "What can I do for you, Juan?"

"A vehicle is in trouble at Khyber Pass." It was the most harrowing stretch of land for miles.

"Over the ledge or in the snowbank?" There was a thin line between those two, a deadly one.

"In the snowbank for now. Cindy Strayer called it in. She's on the way to the doctor with sick babies in the car so she couldn't stop to render aid. I'm tied up on the scene of an eight-car pile-up on the icy underpass. The driver could be in trouble. That's all I know for certain." The weather had been turning. It must already be hitting south of town. "I can't get away for another hour at the least and Mack's trying to help untangle this mess."

Mack Daly owned and operated the town's only towing service. All four of his drivers must be tied up on the Interstate.

"I'll check it out and get word to you." Ash took a final swig of coffee, figuring he needed the added warmth.

"I definitely owe you one for this, Ash."

"It's the least I can do." Juan had connected him to Tony Henson, who'd rented the cabin to Ash, no questions asked. The sheriff was also the reason Ash had found his way to Seven.

So, no, there was no payback needed if Juan asked a favor. Ash ended the call promising to figure out a way Juan could repay him. A debt Ash had no intention of collecting.

Ash handed the phone back to Kat. "Thank you for the hospitality."

She didn't immediately reach for it. "Why don't you keep it? Might make it easier to get word back."

Taking that phone was a slippery slope. At present, Ash needed nothing but a warm place to rest his head, a meal and his dog. He didn't want to get used to depending on anything else.

"Nah. Might just be an abandoned vehicle. This is most likely a precautionary check. With the storm rolling in, I'd hate for someone to be caught unaware. If there is someone inside the vehicle, I'll give him or her a ride to your place to bunk for the night until this whole storm blows over and the vehicle can be dug out tomorrow. Mack is busy. By the time he can help, the storm will keep him away."

"What if the driver is injured? Doesn't hurt to have a phone for emergencies." Kat's smile was warm. Her heart was in the right place. Her pale blue eyes hinted at the beautiful woman she'd been in her day. A woman who'd most likely been used to getting what she wanted by batting those lashes.

Ash chuckled. He flexed his right hand, making as tight a fist as he could manage.

He kept a first aid kit in the glove box. Again, old habits die hard and a good soldier was ready for anything. Ash wasn't so sure about the 'good soldier' part despite being decorated but he was always ready. "I have enough training to field dress any injuries if that's the case. It's probably just a tourist who took the hill for granted, lost control and ended up in a ditch. I'll most likely be back in twenty minutes with a patron."

"I'll keep the coffee pot on."

"Come on, boy." Seven had returned, standing next to Ash's feet. At twelve-years-old he'd worked longer than most in his field. He'd picked up a few injuries along the way. The senior animal moved gracefully but slowly, a ghost of the top-notch bomb sniffer he'd once been. Suited Ash fine. He could relate to Seven. on a soul level. They'd both brought home scars inside and out from the war. They both did the best they could with what they had to work with after. And they'd become each other's lifeline in the past eight months since Seven had come to live with Ash.

Kat shoved a fistful of twenties toward Ash before he could get out the door.

"This is too much." He knew better than to ask where she got the money. Or why she always insisted on paying with cash. Did she stash it under the mattress? That concerned Ash. If he could figure out her money stash so could a random person with bad intentions. Plus, where'd she get all that money? Business had been slow this winter.

"Any other contractor would charge me twice as much and you know it." She made a humph noise.

"I'm not licensed. There's a difference."

"Only 'difference' I see is the quality of work. Yours far exceeds Harlan's." She made another one of those noises. "And who else would be willing to come back with me the minute I drive up with a problem?"

"You could just call most people." Ash didn't own a cell phone. Had no plans to buy one, either. All he needed was a P.O. Box so his government checks could be mailed. He kept his box a couple of towns over, figuring not even his old employer needed to be able to pinpoint his exact location.

He was proud of his service to his country—except the part about helplessly watching his best friends die—and he was done. The men who'd become his only family were gone.

Ash had no plans to get close enough to anyone else to care one way or the other.

CHAPTER 2

EMERY FREEMONT THREW her shoulder into the driver's side door of the rented sedan as she tugged on the handle one more time. Aside from a raging shot of pain on her left side, there was no give.

This wasn't supposed to be happening. None of it. Emery shouldn't be stuck in a damn snowbank in Colorado instead of at home in Texas grading high school science tests. She shouldn't be on the run from a murderer. And she sure as hell shouldn't have had to bury her baby sister.

Icy tendrils wrapped around Emery's spine. Fear was quickly replaced by anger.

The seatbelt was tight across her chest, locked. She couldn't move it enough to wiggle out and climb onto the passenger side. Airbags had deployed. Powder had burned her hands. Her right hand had taken the brunt of the injuries when she'd locked it against the steering wheel as the vehicle spun out of control after hitting an ice patch.

Pain radiated up her elbow and her wrist was already swelling.

Driving the rest of the way to the small town near Glenwood Springs without the use of her dominant hand would be a challenge. But then, that assumed she *actually* survived being stranded and alone in what was supposed to be the worst snow storm of the season. Emery gripped the steering wheel with her good hand. It would take more than a snowbank, freezing cold weather and a bad hand to stop her from finding answers that had cost her baby sister's life.

Tears pricked the backs of Emery's eyes. She'd be damned if she cried.

Even though the Feds couldn't keep Becca safe, Emery couldn't help but feel like she'd let her baby sister down. It didn't matter that Becca was a grown woman capable of making her own decisions. A woman who kept everything hidden. A woman who didn't like anyone interfering with her life.

Emery had known something was up over the

holidays. She should've forced Becca to talk instead of waiting until her sister came to her senses.

Emery smacked her palm against the steering wheel and immediately withdrew her right hand. The pain vibrated up to her elbow but kept her mind off the cold.

Emery had always watched over her younger sister. She'd always been the responsible one between the two of them.

Looking out the driver's side window was no good unless she wanted to stare in the face of a snowbank. The car had launched into a spin then pitched when it hit pavement. The rental had landed cockeyed. There might be enough room for her to squeeze out if she could get the damn door open. Forget the issue of the seatbelt, she'd gnaw that sucker off if it meant her freedom.

Getting over Khyber Pass before the weather turned was a plan that had bit the dust. The rental's navigation system hadn't prepared her for the ice patch on the south-exposed side of the winding mountain pass and only one car had driven by without stopping in the past half hour. Waiting for another one at this rate could prove deadly. Her hands were already numb. If the storm got as bad as predicted, Emery's chances of surviving the night with a half tank of gas pinned inside the vehicle with no access to food or water seemed slim.

Of course, she wouldn't starve or dehydrate right away. That would take days. It occurred to Emery it could take that long to clear the roads after a bad storm.

Forget the fact that she hadn't worn a coat or gloves. But then, she'd had to leave Texas in too big a hurry to be concerned with packing her bag. She'd thrown a few things into an overnighter within minutes.

Growing up in Texas, she had plenty of experience with nasty thunderstorms and tornado warnings but none whatsoever with snow storms. Underestimating the road could be a deadly, she realized.

Emery had to survive. She had to find evidence to put Wren behind bars. Becca deserved justice dammit.

The hum of an engine hit her with a fresh shot of adrenaline. If she could get out of the damn vehicle, she might be able to wave the driver down. It wouldn't do any good to flash her high beams in the snow bank. Oh, she could tap her brakes, but then she'd have to hope for the best.

Out of the rearview, she saw bright red pickup

truck pull onto the side of the road. Hope blossomed for the first time since this whole trip began.

An inappropriate trill of awareness skittered through her when she got a good look at the driver. He climbed out of the driver's seat and stood to his full height. He had to be no less than six feet four inches. He was athletic, all muscle and grace in his jacket and Stetson. It was probably the cowboy hat that hit her with the word *home* when she got a good look at him.

She waved her arms and pumped the brakes a couple more times, so he would know for certain there was a person inside. She remembered the horn and honked it a couple of times.

The temperature was dropping, the air had developed teeth and the cold was starting to bite. She'd been rationing her gas for the worst-case scenario so she could have heat during the night. The cab of the vehicle felt more like the walk-in freezer at her first restaurant job.

At least a hundred-pound German shepherd darted from around the back of the stranger, making a beeline toward her vehicle. The sight of the large animal caused her heart to pound against her ribs. She'd grown up in the city and without pets.

She started the engine and rolled down the

passenger window, ignoring the fact she was shivering.

Nose to the ground, the animal made it to her vehicle first. He went to the trunk first before lunging at her window and barking.

"Seven. Stop." The man's deep baritone sent a shot of warmth through her.

Still, the dog scared the bejesus out of her. Every muscle in her body tensed.

Her rescuer took a few more steps before opening the passenger door. "Are you injured?" The face that came into view caused an unnerving reaction in her stomach. A dozen butterflies released at the granite jawline, dark-haired, steel-eyed features. Most women would consider this man sex-in-a-bucket good-looking and she wouldn't argue. His thick sooty lashes framed serious eyes that she could stare into far longer than what would be considered appropriate.

"Your dog is scaring me." She blinked to break eye contact, lowered her gaze and lifted her right hand toward him with her palm up as he apologized.

The dog paced back and forth. His face alert and body at attention.

"He needs to search your vehicle."

"What?"

"It'll only take a second." The stranger's eyes said there was more to the story.

If she wanted out of this car, she needed to cooperate. She nodded. "Does he bite?"

"Not if I'm around." Not exactly the reassurance she was hoping for.

The vehicle dipped under the dog's weight as he entered the vehicle. The best she could tell from his actions and the seriousness of his expression as he worked he was some kind of police dog.

More of that panic seized her. "Do you work for the law?"

"Not me. Ex-military. So's my dog here. His name is Seven." As promised, the dog finished his work quickly and exited the vehicle.

Emery blew out the breath she'd been holding. "My wrist might be broken and I can't get out of this seatbelt."

"Can you tell me what day it is?" His steel gaze scanned her face, her body. He was most likely checking for injuries but the perusal felt strangely intimate.

Emery tamped down her physical reaction to man who'd taken a knee and wedged himself inside the opened door. His presence sent warmth shooting through her but everything in his eyes said he was off-limits.

"Thursday." That was easy. She'd buried her sister yesterday, on Wednesday.

"Date?"

That one she'd have to think about. "Um," she performed a mental calculation, "February sixth."

A blast of cold air chilled her to the bone, bringing her back to the reality she was trapped inside a car in a coming storm, and she was certain he could hear her teeth chatter.

"Let's get you out of here and somewhere warm." He reached in his back pocket and produced a knife. She noticed he was a lefty as he cut the belt to free her. Thankfully, Seven stayed at his master's side. She had to give it to his training; the animal was well-behaved.

Warmth sounded like heaven. The rest not so much. She'd alerted the car rental company to the fact that she'd been in a wreck and they'd warned her the weather was about to turn and there was no way they could get someone out with a new car before it hit.

With nowhere to go, she didn't have the first clue where to tell him to drop her.

"I'll help you climb over the seat and crawl out on this side. I'm Ash, by the way. Ash Cage."

"Emery Freemont. Thank you for stopping. I'm not sure what I would've done if you hadn't." She lifted her elbow and awkwardly maneuvered her torso toward Ash. He shifted, taking her weight like she was a feather. At five feet six with curves, she'd never been considered a waif, too clumsy to be considered athletic.

Before she could mention her innate fear of dogs, she was back-peddling out of the driver's seat and landing on Ash's lap. His body was hard muscle and warmth. She tensed against him.

"He's trained." She figured it was best to blame the dog instead of own up to the fact that her ramrod straight body came from her back landing against his solid muscle of a chest. She was also sitting in his lap. Her bottom pressed against his most intimate muscle caused her heart to jolt out of the starting gate.

"Seven, out." The dog responded immediately, backing up a couple of paces. It was enough for her to clear the sedan without coming into contact with the animal. His serious brown eyes took her in and she had the sense the dog could see right through her.

He wasn't the only one.

Emery pushed off with her left hand and the strong hand wrapped around her right elbow guided her until she got her balance on the fresh snow. A thick blanket covered a sky that had been bright blue only minutes before. It was safe to say the storm had arrived.

Ash opened the passenger door of Tabasco for Emery, trying to forget just how right she'd felt in his arms as he'd helped her out of the wrecked sedan. The damage to her vehicle meant it wasn't going anywhere until the storm passed.

She immediately climbed in and rubbed her left hand against her arm, trying to stave off the cold. She was still shivering and he could hear her teeth chattering as he offered his coat for warmth.

"I can't take your only coat."

"I'm still warm from the heater."

She nodded, so he draped it around her shoulders. He cranked up the heater and retrieved the spare blanket he kept stashed behind the seat.

"This should help." He unfolded the wool.

She reached for it before he was done, and their hands touched as he handed it to her. A jolt of electricity sizzled across his skin and up his arm. He chalked the out-of-place attraction up to going too long without female companionship. Dating had been the least of his least priorities after settling into Hero's Junction last year; making sense of his life trumped cozy dinners out and hot nights wrapped in the sheets with a leggy blond. Ash smirked. The last part didn't sound so bad.

Ash glanced at her finger. There was no ring, and no line where a band used to be. Relief he had no right to own washed over him.

"Are you passing through town?" Seven dutifully settled into the space behind Ash's seat after sniffing the vehicle for explosives.

"On my way west." The words came out unsteady. She'd passed his very basic field concussion test. A hint of...was that fear?...in her voice might have something to do with taking a ride from a complete stranger.

"There's an inn twenty minutes from here if you need a place to bunk down for the night."

Silence sat between them a few beats longer than

it should've. Something he couldn't quite put his finger on didn't sit right.

"Can you give me a ride into town instead? I'll figure it out from there." It could've been the cold causing her voice to shake but instinct told him there was more to the story.

"I could do that. No problem." There was something haunting in those cinnamon eyes of hers.

"My bag's in the backseat."

Ash jogged over to the vehicle, grabbed the overnight bag and placed it in the back of the cab. "That all you brought with you?"

"Yes." The fact she didn't seem ready to explain herself would normally send up an alarm but there was something warm, intelligent and honest about Emery. Something he didn't want to be drawn toward.

He reclaimed his seat on the driver's side.

"Here's the thing. By the time we get to town, everything will be closed. There won't be so much as a bag of chips left to buy at the corner store because everyone's expecting a bad storm. If Cindy's kids hadn't been sick and needing to go to the doctor you would've been stranded here until the storm let up and the roads cleared. Probably three days, give or take." Her eyes grew wider with each word. If he had to scare her with the truth to knock some sense into her so be it.

"Well, maybe, I-uh-I—"

"You're welcome to stay the night at my place—"

"Okay." Her answer came out faster than a prize thoroughbred through the gate on race day.

"The cabin isn't much. There's a fireplace and a small kitchen." If he could call it that. He'd heard someone use the term, *kitchenette*, before and that sounded about right.

"Is there a warm shower and a couch or chair to sleep on?" She blinked those cinnamon eyes at him and his chest squeezed. "I don't want to put you out."

"You won't. The place is cozy and comfortable." He'd worked on making the place feel like home even though he was fully aware it was a temporary arrangement. The cabin was too run down to rent to skiers but its location was golden, situated between the inn and the resort. Even though he'd grown fond of Kat, Hero's Junction would never be home. Once summer hit, he'd move on.

Ash looked up at the sky, forcing his gaze away from Emery's thick mane of russet locks, and then navigated Tabasco onto the road.

"Which side of the Pass is your place on?"

"West. Why?" He'd chalked her wild eyes and worry lines up to the accident until now.

"No reason." The words came out in a forced casual tone. He'd heard it many times before in people who were scared or up to no good. He wasn't concerned for his safety. She posed no threat to a trained soldier who could get by on twenty-minute naps for days on end.

"We should have your wrist checked out in—"

"No. It'll be fine. I can ice it once we get to your place." She sure seemed eager not to come in contact with anyone else but him. He could tell by the way she grimaced when she thought he wasn't looking she was in serious pain.

"First things first, let's get you warm. We can talk about the rest later." If the storm packed the punch the weatherman thought it would there'd be plenty of time to get to know each other better. His chest tightened at the thought of spending time with Emery. She was beautiful. He'd give her that. Any man with good taste would find her attractive. But looks alone had never done the trick for Ash; there was nothing worse than waking up next to a beauty with no brains. Smart women were sexy as hell.

She adjusted her glasses with her left hand. If she couldn't do that simple act with her right hand her wrist was likely in worse shape than she wanted to let on. Shock coupled with the cold would keep the pain at bay for now. She was in for a surprise later. One he'd hopefully help her avoid.

Ash couldn't ignore the gut instinct that she was in some kind of trouble. Asking her outright could cause her to bolt. He knew what it was like to need help but not be willing or able to ask for it. The shivering woman in the seat next to him brought out his protective instincts—instincts that hadn't failed him in thirty-four years. He didn't figure they'd start now.

Besides, she was injured. She seemed vulnerable. Helping her was like finding a wounded bird. He'd offer the same kind of help to her that he would any injured creature—he'd give her a place to rest and recoup before sending her on her way.

Ash had noticed how quickly she'd jumped at the chance to stay with him even though she was afraid of dogs.

Seven picked up on the scent of fear and adrenaline like no other dog he'd seen. Seven's ears were tilted forward. His serious brown eyes intent on Emery.

A thick blanket of graying clouds covered the skies. Not a hint of blue in sight.

His passenger's stomach growled.

"When's the last time you had something to eat?"

"Last night, I guess." She guessed? She was either in a hurry to get somewhere or on the run. The first thought that struck him...an abusive husband. Ash white-knuckled the steering wheel.

"Think I'll be able to get back on the road by morning?" Ash risked a glance. For the most part, he was able to get a read on people. Chalk it up to his training, he'd developed damn good instincts. She didn't come across like the type who'd commit a serious crime.

First of all, she'd be more prepared. The rental car was a giveaway. If she was attempting to do something illegal the rental agency could track her movements. Only an idiot or a novice would leave a trail so easy to follow.

"Everything okay?"

"What do you mean by that?" Her defensive tone sent more mixed signals. Emery Freemont was a puzzle.

"If you need to get somewhere it might be faster to book a flight."

"Oh, no. Thank you. I can't do that." He was back to the on-the-run theory. Her broken wrist could've come from something besides the wreck. Anger

29

licked through his veins at the thought she might be running from a boyfriend or spouse. "I'll be fine driving."

"I'm sure the rental agency will get a new vehicle to you as soon as the roads clear."

She mumbled something. He could've sworn he heard her say it might be too late. She could have a sick relative.

"Heading to see family?"

"No. I'm on a family errand, though. Sort of." Hesitation in those last two words said he'd struck a nerve.

"Must be important if it can't wait a couple of days until the roads clear."

"Not really." She turned toward the passenger door and fixed her gaze out the window. Hell on a stick if a wall didn't just come up between them.

The mystery beauty had a secret. One she wasn't eager to share. The challenge in her eyes when he turned off the road onto the gravel drive leading to his place warned him to drop the subject.

Interesting. Hell if he'd be able to leave it alone. Those frightened eyes would haunt him the rest of his days if he didn't get to the bottom of what was wrong.

A deeper drive, one he didn't want to acknowledge, had him wanting to fit the puzzle pieces together on Emery Freemont.

For now, he'd give himself the excuse of simply wanting to help a stranger. He might not *know* her, but there was something familiar about Emery. Something he couldn't shut off so easily.

CHAPTER 3

EMERY NEEDED Ash Cage to stop asking questions she couldn't answer. Thankfully, she'd caught herself before blurting out that her sister had been murdered. There was something disarming about the man underneath the black Stetson but letting her guard down would be a costly mistake. Letting the news slip would invite too many questions and allowing him to help would only put him in danger.

Granted, the man was all muscle and intelligence. Everything about him said he could handle himself no matter what came his way.

The minute Emery had realized her sister had been murdered she ditched her own cell phone. Becca had been clear. Don't trust the government.

The Feds would be able to use GPS to track her. Don't trust Wren, the real estate investor she'd fallen for in a whirlwind romance.

The burn phone she'd bought at a convenience store off the highway didn't have GPS. Even if it did, no one knew it was hers now. The phone was too basic to give her details about the weather or anything else useful for her trip, like her smart phone would've. The rental car she'd bribed her neighbor to rent on her behalf had navigation in the form of pre-loaded maps. Those had been pretty basic and did nothing to warn her of how bad the weather would turn.

Snow was already a thick blanket on the ground and there was no end in sight. Her right wrist was a constant throb. She tried not to focus on the pain.

Being without her own cell caused the stress spot in her right shoulder to flare. Emery shoved the unproductive thoughts aside. Her sister was gone…

Becca. Emery fought the hot tears pricking the backs of her eyes. Before the murder, Becca had given Emery a code. She'd warned her sister to be careful. Emery had no idea what she'd find when she arrived at 224 Wickland Street now.

Emery cursed the tragedy. She cursed the

weather. And she cursed Wren for taking her baby sister from her.

The brakes on the truck squeaked. The vehicle came to a stop. The crank of the parking gear being engaged shook Emery from her revelry. She realized she'd been too distracted with her thoughts to watch the road. How would she navigate back down if she couldn't remember how to get back?

A log cabin that was more the size of a shack took up the windshield. She needed to get her bearings. "Anyone else live around here?"

Ash shot her an annoyed look, like she'd just accused him of being a serial killer. "You'll be safe with me if that's what you're asking."

"I wasn't worried." She was more concerned about nosy neighbors than she was about him taking advantage of her. She should fear him. He was linebacker big, with muscles for days. He was also drop-dead, weak-at-the-knees gorgeous. She had no doubt women would line up to date him. He was out of her league. And yet, in an alternate universe she could see herself wanting to get to know him better.

She'd always been smart instead of athletic and curvy as opposed to thin or muscled. Becca had the long, lithe runner's build with legs that went on for days. Emery was five-feet-four-inches on a good day with shoes on.

"It's not much but it'll keep the cold out." He put the ignition in park and cut off the engine. "Hold tight. I'll come around and get the door for you."

With the condition of her right hand she couldn't argue. "I appreciate your kindness. Thank you for giving me a place to sleep tonight."

"You're welcome."

A pair of serious brown eyes stared up at her. Panic made the air thin as she took Ash's extended hand.

"He's a good dog. He won't hurt you."

Ash didn't pull away as she swiveled her legs onto the cold earth. A gust of wind cut right through her coat. She'd been in such a hurry to leave Texas that she hadn't packed a proper coat.

Did she even have one?

Winters in North Texas could have cold snaps. They didn't last.

"Is this all you brought?" His dark brow arched as he angled his head toward the overnight bag in the back.

"Yes."

"What about a coat and gloves?"

"I go from garage to garage where I'm from. It

never stays cold for long in Texas." Damn. She didn't mean to let that slip.

"Texas? Whereabout?" Something dark registered in his deep timbre. Under different circumstances she'd like find out more about Ash. Figure out why the mention of her home state brought out pain in his voice and in his eyes.

"The Metroplex. You?" She didn't exactly give away her location. The Metroplex covered a wide area, including Dallas, Forth Worth and a dozen suburbs like Arlington and McKinney. The population was six and a half million.

"Small town south of Austin by the name of Gunner. Not much to look at but cattle."

She shivered against the cold. Something in his eyes said the subject was closed.

"Let's get you inside."

The cabin had a stone path leading up to a small porch. A pair of unfinished rocking chairs in various stages of refurbishing nestled together with what looked like a hand-carved side table in between.

"Did you make that?" Emery tried to distract herself from the pain pulsing up her right arm from her wrist.

"It's a work in progress."

Ash opened the door, she noted, without a key.

Being from a major metropolitan city she always locked the door. The only time she didn't was to check the mail and that was literally ten steps from the front porch of her rented townhouse, and at night she set an alarm. She'd regretted not getting an animal for protection after reading a dog was the number one deterrent for burglars. Ever since the neighbor's terrier bit her when she was six years old she'd been petrified of all dogs.

"He has a routine that he has to follow." He held the door open and the dog darted inside first. Nose to the floor, he searched every inch of the place.

"Excuse the mess. I wasn't expecting company."

"A hot shower and warm bed are pretty much all I need to be happy." It occurred to her that might be difficult to manage with one arm.

He glanced at her wrist, which throbbed. "Ice and compression are your new best friends."

The log cabin consisted of two rooms; a kitchen-dining room and the living-sleeping space. The bed sat in the right-hand corner in an alcove. It couldn't be more than full-size and she couldn't imagine a man of Ash's build fitting comfortably.

She eyed the comfortable-looking leather loveseat. "I'll sleep there."

Privacy would be nice. Not because she feared

Ash would do something inappropriate in the middle of the night. She had other plans—plans that involved slipping out before dawn. Ash seemed like a decent person. One who didn't deserve to be dragged into her family's tragedy.

Don't get her wrong, she'd been on her own for so long it would be nice if someone had her back for a change. Lonely didn't begin to describe birthdays and Christmas. Working long hours left her little time for a social life.

"I'll take the couch. You're on the bed." He motioned toward an alcove. "Make yourself at home while I get us some heat." Ash went to work, making a fire in the fireplace.

"Is he finished?" Seven was at Ash's side.

"Yes."

"Why does he do that?"

"He's retired military, a bomb sniffer."

"Is that what you did?" She shouldn't ask questions. Getting to know each other wasn't a smart move. In fact, the less she knew about the handsome stranger the better.

"Not me. I just got lucky and adopted him after his retirement. His handler couldn't take him."

The second thing Emery noticed, no TV. It shouldn't strike her as odd but it did. Every male apartment she'd visited during her 29 years of life had a massive TV as the focal point of the room. There were other items missing here at the cabin, like a black-and-white Ansell Adams photo. It was another staple of a male dwelling if there was anything on the wall at all. The color scheme was generally black-and-white, the décor urban.

In this space, the love seat was a made of a warm brown leather material. Across from it, where most men would've placed a massive flat screen TV, was a stone fireplace instead.

There was a small kitchen area and a table with two chairs, and a door that she assumed led to the bathroom. At least, she prayed there was indoor plumbing. The thought of an outhouse in the freezing cold made her shiver even more.

This place was barely big enough for a man of Ash's size and yet it somehow suited him. Although the kitchen wasn't big it had everything needed, a coffee maker, a small refrigerator and a stovetop. There was nothing pretentious about the cabin and even though there were no personal belongings, like photos he made it feel homey with his presence. His warm, spicy, outdoor-campfire scent filled the place, warming her in places that had long been iced over.

Two people and a dog in the space should've felt cramped. Instead, it felt cozy.

Emery wouldn't call the place modern. She would call it clean and comfortable. And except for the small size, it seemed to fit Ash's low-key personality. It had that worn glove feeling her dad had often talked about when she was a kid.

Once the two chairs on the patio were finished and a few odds and ends projects that seemed to be in progress, she could see him making a home here. The place was made of logs. The roof out of tin, extending out over the patio. It was the kind of place she envisioned a couple sitting outside on a warm summer evening with a glass of wine.

"Your home is lovely." Why did saying the home out loud cause more tears to prick the backs of her eyes?

"Not mine."

"Let me take a closer look at that wrist." Ash walked over to Emery with athletic grace, and she held out her wrist for his inspection. "How much pain are you in?"

"Enough to notice," she said with a frown.

"I have a few more supplies in the bathroom. Hold on." Ash disappeared into the adjacent room, leaving the door open and the light on. Being able to keep him in sight allowed her shoulder muscles to un-bunch a little. He returned a few seconds later and produced a red box with a white cross over top of it, a first aid kit.

"This might be better if we sit and you can rest your arm on something." He glanced around the small space before his gaze landed on the two-top in the dining nook.

She took the seat opposite him before extending her arm across the table. It dawned on her that he might have a girlfriend or wife. She glanced at his ring finger. Relief flooded her when there was no gold band. That didn't mean he wasn't attached thought; a gorgeous man like him had to have someone in the wings.

"Will your wife be joining us later?" Emery told herself the question was pure survival and nothing personal. She needed to know how many folks she might come into contact with, who might be able to give her description to Wren or to the Feds who would then leak it to the jerk.

If Wren knew where Emery was he might just figure out where she was headed. Her pulse sped up, tattooing its beat against her skin, waiting for his answer.

Ash screwed up his face, didn't look up from his

work as he wrapped a flexible material from her elbow to her hand. "No wife. No girlfriend. Just me and Seven. And we like it best that way."

Good didn't sound right to say but she was relieved. A few more butterflies released in her stomach at the admission.

CHAPTER 4

ASH KEPT one eye on Emery while he wound the bandage around her arm. She was in enough pain without him adding to it. There was a fine balance between applying enough pressure to help her, and hurting her wrist further.

"This should help stabilize your wrist." He'd cut a paper towel roll in half and then split the cardboard tube down the middle into another two pieces. He taped one of the pieces to her wrist before wrapping it; he was getting better every day at using his left hand. "Tell me if I press too hard."

"It's good." She winced.

"It's not too tight?"

"No. Moving it hurts like hell but this is actually helping."

"Hold on." Next, he made an ice pack and gingerly placed it on top. "I'll let you take it from here."

She'd asked about a wife. He'd given her more information than she'd asked for in an attempt to gain her trust. This was as good a time as any to turn the tables. "How about you? Got anyone back home you need to check in with?" It was most likely protective instinct on overdrive that had him needing to make sure a boyfriend or husband hadn't done this to her, hadn't put the fear in her eyes.

"No. There's no one special. I live alone." The table top suddenly became real interesting to her. "You said this place is a rental. Have you lived here long?"

"Eight months give or take." He didn't mind giving up a little information about himself if it meant gaining ground with her. "My time in the service ended with an IED." He flexed his right hand. "Military thought I should go home considering I lost nerve function. This seemed like as good a place as any to lay my hat until I could figure out my next move."

"Have you?"

He cocked an eyebrow in response.

"Figured out what you want to do next?"

"Not yet." He could admit to feeling restless in Hero's Junction. It wasn't a surprise. No place would ever feel like home. Texas was part of his past—a painful past. Technically he knew he was done there, but Texas had always been home. That land... He'd always loved the land and being away left a hole in his chest. Damned if he could go back again. He'd tried but withdrew from town further and further until one day he stared at a plane ticket, unable to use it.

Somehow, it wasn't right that he could when three of his best friends—friends who'd become brothers and the only family he had to speak of—would never set foot in the Lone Star State again. And then there was Rachel Lee, his girlfriend. His *former* girlfriend. The *Dear John* letter she'd sent him after his friends died had been salty icing on top of a cake made with bad eggs. "You want coffee?"

"Yes."

"How do you take yours?" He stood, crossed the room and made quick work of the pot on counter. It was the old-fashioned kind, no pods. Just good old-fashioned coffee grounds.

"If you have a little milk that'd be great. If not, I can take it black."

"Milk it is." He fixed two mugs and set them down on the table.

"Thank you for everything you've done today."

"Folks help each other around here." He shrugged it off like it was no big deal. And it wasn't.

"Did you know someone here?"

"I wandered around for a few days. I knew I wanted to be in Colorado. I just didn't know where when I first got here. There's a ski resort not too far from here. Town in the other direction. Figured it wouldn't be too hard to get work, so I settled here after staying at a roadside inn and receiving the best hospitality I could imagine.

She motioned toward the dog at Ash's side. "How'd you two end up together?"

"My friend knows the sheriff." Ash took note of the way Emery bristled when he mentioned the law. "Juan knew a guy by the name of Joseph Kuntz. Kujo, that's what they called him, had been in similar circumstances when he'd shown up in Colorado. He was a handler who worked Delta Force, also medically boarded out. Kujo reunited with his dog, Six, who turns out is Seven's cousin. He told me about Seven and I headed to San Antonio to make the request. His handler is still on active duty for another three years and Seven needed a good home."

After a week-long trip to Lockland to fill out paperwork, Ash and Seven had returned to Colorado, their new home. A new state for a new life.

"Does he always check a place before he enters? Even home?"

"It's one of his many quirks."

"It must be hard for Seven to be a working dog, especially now that he's a civilian."

"The adjustment hasn't been easy on him but we're figuring it out as we go."

She took another sip of coffee. "Did you grow up around animals?"

"My best friend's family owned a ranch. But they were barn animals. Aside from food and water, they took care of themselves."

"What about Kujo and Six? Do they live nearby?"

"He moved to the Crazy Mountains of Western Montana to work for Brotherhood Protectors." Seven and his cousin Six had never met, even though both had been whelped in Germany. Both had spent their first year of life there, which explained why they both responded best to German commands. The main difference was that Kujo had been Six's handler while Ash and Seven had never met before summer.

Ash tried to pick up his mug. Tremors started in his right hand. Damn, nerves.

Emery watched. She seemed like she wanted to ask what happened and then decided against it. She made a move for her mug with her right hand and winced. It took a second before she awkwardly lifted her mug in her left. "The next few days are going to be tricky."

"You might want to get an X-ray."

"What can they do? If it's a fracture they'll wrap it and send me home."

"I have a couple of ibuprofen," he retrieved a pair along with a glass of water. "You should eat something with them."

"Thank you. Again. I appreciate your hospitality." There was a genuine quality to her voice. "I'm not sure what I would do or where I'd be right now if not for you."

She flashed her eyes at him and her cheeks turned a darker shade of pink. Ash didn't want to notice how much it highlighted the vibrant color in her green eyes.

Ash moved to the fridge. "I have fruit. Apples and oranges. I'm not much in the kitchen but can make a mean turkey sandwich."

"I'm not sure I could eat." He'd heard her stomach growl earlier. She had to be hungry.

"We could share one. I have soup. Kat makes a pot every week and sends some home with me." Again, she fixed her gaze on the table.

"Okay."

He pulled out ingredients, made the sandwich and then heated the soup. His right hand trembled when he set down her plate.

"Mind if I ask what happened?" She picked up her half of the sandwich and took a bite.

"Permanent nerve damage. Sometimes it works. Sometimes not. Damn thing has a mind of its own." That's as much as he could tell her about the incident that had cost him dearly. He'd spent weeks in rehab, wishing for a different outcome.

"I'm sorry." Her soft-spoken voice had a musical quality to it that could be addictive. Under different circumstances, he reminded. Picking up a stranded woman with an injured wrist who seemed ready to jump if he said *Boo* wasn't exactly good timing for the attraction hitting him square in the chest.

"It gave me a reason to think of something else to do with my life besides career military."

"Wasn't there a desk job you could do? It seems

49

extreme to walk away from your profession because you got hurt."

"There were other factors." If she hadn't taken a sip of coffee and looked at him with such expectant eyes he would've ended the conversation right then and there. Even Kat couldn't get him to talk about the real reason he took the walk. "I lost friends."

She apologized again in a way that sounded comforting. He appreciated her for not patronizing him or looking at him with pity. None of those emotions would bring his buddies back.

"Is that why you came here instead of going home?" She moved her hand and winced. "Sorry. You don't have to answer. It's none of my business and I shouldn't have—"

"In a manner of speaking, yes." Talking to her was easy. It was probably just the lost look deep in her cinnamon eyes that he could relate to. "We were called the Texas Boys. It didn't seem to matter that I was from Gunner, Mack was from McKinney, Tommy was from Bedford. We didn't know each other before we signed up and had no idea how we ended up in the same unit."

"Fate?"

"Some people called it that. We probably were meant to be friends. Mack had this thick accent. He grew up as wild and free as the horses on his family's ranch. Tommy's hometown was near the airport. He planned to go home and marry his high school sweetheart after he saved enough money to set them up on a small property. She was obsessed with Alpacas. He wanted to give her everything she wanted and more." He coughed to clear the emotion gathering in his chest. "They were good men."

"They sound like it. I would've liked to have met them." When he looked up at her, a mix of emotion passed behind those cinnamon flecks. Sadness? Loneliness? Regret?

"Those boys were the only family I had left."

She took a sip of coffee and looked around. He could see water pooling in her eyes. "I can see why you decided to stick around here. This place is perfect."

"It suits my needs for now." Using his left hand, he picked up his spoon and took a bite of soup. "Is your family still in Texas?"

She shook her head. Her lips thinned. Her gaze focused on the brown liquid in her cup. "I had a sister. She passed away."

When her gaze flicked down and to the left, Ash caught onto the fact she wasn't being completely honest. Experience had taught him a thing or two about when someone was covering the truth. The emotion in her voice was clear. Emery had a sister. One she seemed to love very much.

Something was off. What about her sister was she hiding?

"I'm sorry for your loss."

She blinked up at him and he realized her grief was fresh. Since she would be up and out as soon as the storm cleared he figured it wouldn't hurt to ask a few questions. Talking had never really been his forte until her. He *liked* talking to Emery. "You two were close?"

She nodded before turning her head and wiping a stray tear from her cheek. "Our parents died in a car crash when I was nineteen. I was still living at home, working and taking night classes at a local college. My sister and I were devastated. We were a close-knit family, always just the four of us. My mom had family in Texas who never spoke to us because they didn't like the way she handled their mother's funeral from years back." She paused. "Families can be complicated."

"I hear that, which is why I never wanted one of my own." A small piece of him he'd buried long ago surfaced, reminding him he'd wanted those things at one time. A long time ago, the annoying voice reminded.

"My sister, who was seventeen at the time, took an after-school job and finished high school. I kept taking classes until I finished with my degree and became a teacher. Becca, that's my sister's name, was always the fun sister. She was the one who took risks. That's exactly what she did when she met," she glanced up, "her last boyfriend."

The way her voice trailed off at the end said she didn't approve of the guy.

Before he could dig deeper, her stomach growled again.

"We should finish eating before the soup gets cold."

"Right." This time he heard relief in her tone, which sent another alarm bell ringing.

Emery's sister was dead. Emery didn't trust the boyfriend. Her earlier questions about whether or not he had a girlfriend or wife made more sense. She was most likely trying to figure out if anyone else would show and then be able to give a description of her.

Normally, the line of questioning would put him on guard, have him wondering what illegal activity she was involved in.

For better or worse, he trusted Emery.

GUILT SHOT HOLES through Emery's chest as she slipped out of the covers in the middle of the night. She'd spent the past ten minutes listening to the soft sound of Ash's steady breathing. She'd waited long enough for her eyes to adjust to the darkness.

Ash slept sitting up on the sofa, his arms folded over his broad chest. Seven curled up next to his master. Leaving without a word stabbed her with more guilt.

The man had been good to her. Better than good. He'd been an angel. He'd taken care of her wrist, given her food, a place to shower and rest—his bed, no less—and here she was about to borrow his truck without permission.

Desperate times called for desperate measures, she thought. She reminded herself that being seen with her could be bad for Ash's longevity.

If Wren was capable of getting to Becca, even with the Feds involved, what hope did anyone else have?

Resolve coiled in her stomach. Becca deserved justice. Emery was willing to risk her life to find answers. But Ash? He had no idea what he was getting himself into and it wasn't fair to put him in danger.

Between Emery and Becca, Emery had always been the rock. She was used to being the strong one. So, it was a shock for Emery to realize how nice it was to have someone else look after her for a change. But that was dangerous.

She tiptoed across the wood floor, gathered her belongings and placed a wad of twenty-dollar bills inside his clean coffee mug sitting on the counter. Leaving money was supposed to ease her conscience, so what was the heavy weight sitting on her chest about?

She whispered an apology before carefully lifting Ash's keys.

Seven perked up. His gaze locked onto her. She froze, willing him to stay put so he wouldn't disturb Ash.

The panic thrummed in her chest, beating against her ribs like a two-year-old who'd gotten ahold of a drum set—wild and unpredictable.

Emery chanced a few more steps. She risked a glance at the sofa. Relief washed over her the minute she realized Ash was in a deep sleep and Seven didn't seem like he'd expose her.

She was so close to the door handle she could reach out and touch it. A few steps and she'd be out the door and toward freedom. So, why couldn't she force her feet to move?

Guilt weighed her arms, making them too heavy to open the door. She couldn't do it. She couldn't take his vehicle. She couldn't sneak out. She couldn't do that to him.

Ash sat straight up. "Where do you think you're going with my keys?"

A second later, the light flipped on, lighting up the room.

She looked at the metal in her hand. "It's not what you think. Well, actually, it is. But I didn't meant to—"

"What? Steal my truck? Put the damn keys down." There was no other way he would see this situation other than a flat-out betrayal. The fire in his dark eyes shot a warning. She wasn't afraid of him. Not after getting to know him last night. And that made what she was doing that much worse.

Emery set her bag down, walked over and set his keys on the coffee table in front of him. "I woke up and thought it would be best if I left without involving you more in my life."

"What did I say last night that made you think I

wouldn't help?" He covered the hurt in his voice with anger. In fact, the anger came through loud and clear.

"I don't deserve your forgiveness. I won't ask for it." All she could do was apologize. She knew the minute she picked up the keys it had been a bad idea. She twisted her fingers together, ignoring the pain shooting up her arm.

Ash stood to his full height. He practically towered over her and she could feel his presence in the room.

She braced herself for the tongue-lashing she deserved and was out right shocked when she lifted her gaze to meet his and found compassion.

"Did I make a mistake trusting you?"

Even though all evidence pointed to the contrary and she had no idea how to convince him differently, she said, "No."

"Good." He rubbed his eyes with the mules of his hands. "Because my brain doesn't work well without caffeine. If I turn my back are you going to pull something?"

"No."

"Good. You want a cup?" His sleepy voice tugged at her heart.

"Yes." A blast, like the one that had hit her square

in the chest yesterday when she first saw him, slammed into her again. Under different circumstances, she'd like to get to know Ash better, especially after talking to him last night.

The connection she'd felt—still felt—with him was real and not something she'd felt in a very long time if ever.

Her situation was too complicated to get involved with someone, with him. The timing couldn't be worse. An annoying voice reminded her she wouldn't be in his house right now if life hadn't taken a horrible turn.

Emery followed Ash into the kitchen, taking a seat at the two-top. For someone who seemed determined to be alone, she noted the place where he lived was built for two. Did he notice? Would he be too stubborn to admit it if he did?

What did it matter? She'd be long gone and out of his mind forever as soon as he drove her to her vehicle.

"Did you check the temperature outside?" He handed over a steaming mug and all she could think was this man was a saint.

"No."

"So, let me get this straight. You were planning to run off half-cocked after a snow storm in a windbreaker without knowing what you were getting yourself into?" When he put it like that it did sound pretty stupid, and reckless. Emery was normally more practical. Becca had always been the edgy one. The wild one. The fun one?

"I know how this must look—"

"Like someone who needs a hand-up, which I'm willing to give if you'll let me help you." That wasn't the response she expected.

"I'm not used to letting someone hold my hand."

"Shame." He locked gazes and took a sip of coffee.

Her cheeks flamed when he looked at her like he could read her mind. She dropped her gaze to his lips, noticing a small drop of coffee in the corner of his mouth. Leaning across the table to do something about it wasn't an option.

She shouldn't even be noticing his lips or his muscles or the way his voice made her feel like everything might magically turn out all right after all.

"You had my turkey sandwich last night. The other thing I know how to fix is a mean egg. You hungry?" He pushed back from the table and stood up. He walked over to the coffee table then returned and pitched the keys on the two-top. "Might want to get something warm in your stomach before you take off again."

She was already shaking her head. "I can't take your truck. You need that."

"Not as much as you." She couldn't argue his point.

"What will happen? You already said you don't have neighbors around for miles. You'll run out of food. I'm pretty sure no one delivers all the way up here and after a snow storm no less."

The compassionate look on his dark features said he wasn't trying to make her feel bad. "People look after each other here. If I don't turn up at Kat's inn after a day or two for work, she'll send someone up to check on me. I have at least enough food to last until the roads are cleared. Seven has everything he needs right here, clean water and food. We'll be fine."

This time when he looked at her she could see something that looked a lot like hurt in his eyes.

"I've been a pretty bad guest so far." She could risk another day or so. "The rental company should be able to deliver another vehicle. I should just wait."

"Can I ask a question? Why are you in such a hurry? Does it have to do with your sister's death?"

"Yes."

"Do you trust me enough to tell me what happened?"

"It's not you I'm worried about. It's him." The words slipped out before she had a chance to reign them in. She slapped her hand across her mouth like she could stop herself from spilling any more family secrets.

"An ex?"

She slowly lowered her hand, bringing it down to her side.

"My sister's." The truth was that she wanted someone to lean on for a change.

"Was he responsible for her death?" He didn't say the word murder, but it was clear what he meant.

"I believe so. Yes."

"Is that why you don't want to involve me? You're afraid I'll get hurt?" Bingo. She couldn't have said it better herself.

"Yes."

"But he could get to you while you figure out how to make sure he's arrested for his crime?" He turned around and leaned a slender hip against the counter.

"That's right."

"The way I see it you need my help."

"You have a life here. A quiet one. A safe one."

"To hell with safe. Safe isn't the code I live by."

Emery stood and met him halfway in the middle of the room. "I know we haven't known each other for long, but you seem like a really nice guy—"

A grunt tore from his throat. "I'm not a nice guy. I'm a sniper. I'm a former soldier. And I'm pissed that I not only lost the best friends I'll ever have, but my right hand is fucked up for the rest of my life and in my screwed-up head I know I deserve it for being the one to come home."

"And yet you're putting yourself in danger to help a complete stranger." She made eyes at him as though that brought her point home.

He cupped her chin with his hands. His spicy, campfire scent washed over her senses when she took a breath, and warmth pooled in all her feminine places. Her head was dizzy as she tipped her lips the rest of the way toward his.

"Would a nice guy do this?" He brought his lips down on hers. The tender touch turned hungry and needy as she teased his tongue inside her mouth.

Ash groaned against her mouth and she expected him to pull back.

He didn't.

CHAPTER 5

NEED COILED inside Ash's body. He tried not to think about how long it had been since he'd had great sex. Hell, *any* sex.. His body screamed *too long*.

Emery's hands flew to his shoulders and he half expected her to push him away. Instead, her fingers trailed along the muscles of his chest, her palms flattened against him.

He dragged his hands around her waist. Splaying his hands on the small of her back, he hauled her flush with his rigid body. She moaned against his lips causing a trill of awareness to skitter across his flesh.

He pulled back enough to feather a trail of kisses down her neck, stopping against the base of her neck where her pulse pounded erratically. His own breathing came out in rasps. He'd never been this hard or this needy with his clothes still on.

Yeah, it had been too long since he'd found himself in a tangle in the sheets with a beautiful woman. And this felt different. This was also not the time to figure out how or why. He had an urgent need that required his full attention.

He trailed his tongue down the center of her chest. Her back arched, pressing generous breasts toward him, and she moaned when he ran his slick tongue along the edges of her lacy bra. He brought his hand up to cup her breast. Her nipple beaded against his palm, causing another shot of need to render him useless to the urgent need driving through him.

"Are you sure you didn't hit your head in the wreck yesterday?" Her shirt was off and thrown on the floor in a flash. He unhooked her pale pink lacy number. Pink was his new favorite color. He loved the way it had looked against her creamy skin. It joined her shirt a second later.

"Yes. Why?"

"Because I want to make sure you're fully cognizant of what's happening and have no regrets later." Her response came in the form of lifting his chin until he stood at his full height.

Emery locked gazes with him and his heart squeezed when he looked into those cinnamon eyes that had darkened with the same need brewing inside him. "I want to have the hottest sex I've ever had in my life with you right now, Ash. On the floor if need be. I don't care where. Just so long as we're careful with my wrist."

"I can do better than the floor." In one fluid motion, he lifted her off her feet. She wrapped her legs around his midsection, denim grinding against denim, as he walked her to the bed. Her full breasts pressed against the cotton of his t-shirt. He had on entirely too many clothes.

Ash set Emery on the edge of the bed as he shrugged out of his t-shirt. Her good hand was already at the snap on his jeans. Those came off and he started a new pile next to the bed. His boxers were next.

She leaned back and he helped her out of her jeans. Those matching pale pink panties she wore tightened the coil until it felt ready to snap.

All Ash could think was how deep he wanted to bury himself inside her, how much he wanted to get lost in her. He took both hips in his hands and pulled her sweet bottom to the edge of the bed.

Wrapped his hands around her thighs, he determined that he wanted to see her pleasure first. Her back arched and she released a string of sexy moans when he worked his way up the inside of her thigh until he drove his tongue inside her.

He heard his name repeated—loving the sound of it on her lips—as he brought her to the brink of ecstasy before she freefell from the cliff. He loved how responsive her body was to his touch and got one hell of an ego boost out of how fast she'd come for him.

Ash moved to the nightstand and retrieved a condom. He ripped the package open with his teeth, his erection thick with need to be buried inside her.

"Let me do it." She scraped her fingernail across his midsection and then down the trail of hair leading to where he was more than ready for her.

The condom balanced on his tip, she rolled it until it sheathed his length. He stopped for a minute to look at her, *really* look at her and his breath hitched.

"Damn. You're beautiful."

Her cheeks burned red and it made her look even sexier. "I'm n—"

He leaned in and covered her mouth with his before she could protest. She was beautiful in every sense of the word and he'd spend whatever time it took showing her.

When he was sure she was thoroughly out of breath—and therefore couldn't argue—he said the words again, stronger this time.

"I like that you think so." She didn't blush this time. Instead, her gaze stayed locked onto his. "I feel beautiful when you look at me and say it."

"Perfection." He ran his finger along the sweet curve of her hip.

Emery initiated the next kiss and it nearly blew his mind. He cupped her breast in his hand before rolling her nipple in between his thumb and forefinger. It beaded in his hand. *Jesus.*

There was so much more to his attraction to this woman than physical—although, he had that in spades. Intelligent. Strong. Honest. The fact that she was beautiful to boot and didn't seem to realize shred his protective layers. Hell, if he was going down Heartbreak Pass he might as well go all in. One night with Emery wasn't going to be nearly enough. And he'd be lucky if got more than twenty-four hours with her.

Emery tugged him on top of her as she helped her lie back on the bed. Mouths fused, eyes locked, he dipped the tip of his erection in her sweet heat.

Nothing in Ash wanted this moment to fly by. He needed to distract himself from how incredible she felt. Oil change. Sanding the rocking chairs.

None of those thoughts could sidetrack him when she bucked him inside a little deeper. None of those thoughts could force his gaze off her face that was flush with desire, eyes glittery with need as she looked up at him. None of those thoughts could block his ears from hearing her moans of pleasure as he thrust a little deeper.

The fact that she was ready for him, all silk and tension, drove him into a near-frenzy.

He pumped harder and she matched him stride for stride. He loved the way her body moved with his, like two pieces that fit together perfectly. *She* fit him perfectly.

Her reactions caused his body to jump into overdrive.

"Ash," she breathed his name and it was the damn sexiest sound he'd ever heard. "Don't stop."

"Not a chance." He thrust himself deeper and deeper as her muscles constricted around his length.

He could feel the coil tighten those last few notches but was determined to bring her over the edge first.

Deeper. Harder. She grasped at his chest with her

left hand, demanding purchase. Her fingernails dug into his skin. Ecstasy engulfed him. *Not yet, Cage.*

His body drove toward a relentless need for release. She was close. He could see it, feel it, hear it.

As Ash ground his sex into hers a dangerous word popped into his thoughts. *Mine.*

"Ash," she repeated his name a couple more times as she let go, her body a field of electricity and impulse.

With a primal grunt, his body detonated. He flew over the edge and released. This, with Emery, was so much more than the best sex of his life. He was in trouble. Damn good thing he liked trouble.

His chest still heaving, he didn't immediately pull out. He balanced most of his weight on his elbows and knees, not wanting to break the connection with Emery a second sooner than he had to.

She needed to know how he felt about her, so he kissed her with all the tenderness he could manage.

When he finally stopped, it was to catch his breath. He rolled onto his back and wrapped his arm around her, pulling her into the crook where she twined her limbs around him.

"Damn." He couldn't hold in the chuckle that rolled out any more than he could slow his rapid pulse.

"Back atcha." She smiled. He looked at those skilled lips of hers, still swollen from kissing. Need welled up inside him. He'd gone stints without sex before while on a mission, but needing round two before he caught his breath from the first was new.

He took his time making love to her the second time.

"ARE YOU HUNGRY?" She had to be after two solid rounds of smokin' hot sex. Sex, yes. Ash could admit what they'd just experienced was so much more than the act of sex. It had been spiritual. And it changed things between them as far as he was concerned. What that meant exactly was a question for another time.

Ash was too damn happy to get in his own way with depressing thoughts.

When Emery looked up at him, curled around his body, he noticed just how well she fit.

"Do you have to move to get us something to eat?" There was a subtle shift in her tone and in the way she looked at him. He should know, he felt it too.

"Afraid so."

"Then, no." She cracked a smile and he couldn't help but notice how much that small act brightened her face.

Her sense of humor and intelligence made her even sexier.

Now to convince her to stick around.

EMERY FELT the cold sheets the minute Ash left. She watched him, too, all naked and glorious. He was as perfect as she could imagine a man could be, his muscles silk over steel and the definition in those abs alone...practically billboard worthy. And that was only the tip of the iceberg. The man had a few other irresistible traits. He was resourceful, smart, and kind. The Ash Cage package was the real deal.

Ash located his boxers and moved into the kitchen. He walked with athletic grace, like a tiger— strong and assured, with the ease that came with knowing he stood at the top of the food chain.

Her body ached for him to come back to bed. It was a strange sensation considering the fact the only things she knew about him were his name, his address and the fact that he'd served his country.

She blinked up to catch him staring at her, a puzzled look on his face.

"What's wrong?"

"I just had the best sex of my life with a man I met a few hours ago." Surely, he could understand her issue.

"And the problem with that is?" The grin smattered across his face at her admission should make him seem cocky, but it only added to his renegade sex appeal.

She should be embarrassed, but being with Ash felt like the most natural thing. Logically, it made no sense that she'd be drawn to someone so quickly. Her parents had talked about love at first sight and how it had worked for them. Emery never saw it as a possibility for herself because she was too logical, too overly analytical to let her emotions run wild. Her overthinking brain would always get in the way and she'd chalk instant chemistry up to lust and not something that could last. Being able to let go of her emotions and really love someone would take time. Her scars would have to heal.

"You admittedly don't have a phone and I don't see a laptop around. I have to get back on the road soon." She tried to shrug off the pain that came with the realization they'd never see each other again.

"To find out what happened to your sister?" He poured two mugs of coffee, set one on the counter and brought the other to her. In bed. When did that ever happen? She mentally calculated the days when that had happened in her life. Didn't take long to come up with the number zero.

"Yes."

"I'd like to help if you'll let me."

With what just happened between the two of them—and she was still trying to figure out exactly what that was beyond sex because this felt like so much more—she owed him an explanation. "I would accept under normal circumstances. This is too dangerous."

The bold and mischievous look he shot her could melt ice in the dead of an Alaskan winter. "All the more reason you shouldn't be doing it alone."

"We've barely met. I can't let you risk your life for me." She realized the irony in those words the second she thought about his service; he'd literally done just that for her and millions of other Americans he would never meet.

"With all due respect, I'm the one with training."

Hells bells. She couldn't argue there. "True."

His face cracked, a slow grin spread across too white teeth. He seemed to know his argument was making ground. Did he have to look so convincing with those man muscles? She'd already seen how skilled his hands could be in the bedroom, his tongue for that matter and every other part of his body. "I know my way around weapons. I have tactical training."

"We know nothing about each other, Ash. Be reasonable."

"You already know I'm from Texas. My last job was a sniper. I've been out a little more than half a year. My dog's name is Seven. He's the only family I have to speak of and my reason for getting out of bed every morning." He shot a look at her that released a dozen butterflies in her stomach. "I'm hoping that's about to change."

Warmth flooded her. She felt it, too. Whatever 'it' was…the lightning bolt, the tsunami, the shot to the chest. The name didn't matter. The feeling had struck the second she saw him. It was a mix of a thunderclap in her chest and a feeling deep in her stomach—like wow!—that told her to pay extra attention to this man. He was special.

"I can't argue the fact that you have more experience than I do. All I can say is this isn't your battle."

"Tell me something about you. What do you do for a living?"

"I'm a teacher. High school chemistry is my specialty."

His gaze roamed her body with appreciation. "Damn. I'd have paid more attention in class if my high school chemistry teacher looked like you." His smile widened. "Actually, with my hormones raging the way they were at that age, I wouldn't have heard a word you said."

Emery couldn't hold back the laugh bubbling up from her chest. "Now I know why some of my boys are failing."

"By the time they're in high school, they're no longer boys, sweetheart."

He had her there. They were young adults developing into young men—none of which she'd ever thought about in a dating sense nor would she ever. "They'll always be kids to me."

"You already know more about me than anyone here in Hero's Junction. Tell me more about you. What's your favorite color?"

"Purple."

He cocked a brow. "Really?"

"Yes. Pale purple. It's pretty."

He nodded, like he conceded pale purple was a better choice.

"What's yours?"

"It used to be blue like the sky. After last night, it's pink." The laugh that rumbled out of his chest stirred her attraction even more. Her cheeks should flame with embarrassment but there was something about Ash that felt too right. Being with him was...effortless, easy. The best twelve hours of her life.

Her last relationship had been the opposite. When she really thought about it, they all had been. Early on after her parents had died she was too busy working, going to school and watching over Becca to date. The first real relationship Emery had had was with her math professor. A month into it, he picked her up in a minivan after she'd called in a favor because her car wouldn't start.

Chet Haynes tried to sell her on the idea he and his wife were separated. Young and naïve, she'd wanted to believe him. She might've been innocent but she wasn't stupid. A little recon revealed he was very much married with little kids.

Breaking off that relationship had taken all of two seconds. She'd confronted him in front of his wife. The woman needed to know what kind of man she'd married.

"Past relationships?" Emery refocused on the God-like man in the room with her. Something told her that if Ash Cage committed to a woman, there'd be no cheating.

"There've been a few. Nothing significant." He turned the tables. "You?"

"Same." Unless she counted Darren Brinker. The two had dated for a year when she first hired on D.D. Smart High School. The breakup had been amicable and, as it turned out, both had been expecting the other one to be the 'bad' guy. There'd been no spark between them. The best word she could use to describe their relationship was safe.

Silly, that was the one she looked back on from time to time and wondered if she'd been too hasty calling it off. Just looking at him in front of her now made her pulse pound and caused heat to pool between her thighs.

The biggest risk? Her heart. A man like Ash—a man she could really give her whole heart to—could shatter her into a thousand tiny pieces. How would she ever recover?

"We just met. I'll give you that. I know you can feel what's going on between us is different. At least, it is for me."

She nodded.

"There's something special here and we owe it to ourselves to give it a chance."

"That part's tricky with what's going on in my life right now." Tears threatened when she was brought back to reality. "Becca deserves justice."

He finished with the omelets and brought two plates to the two-top. "Why not go to the sheriff?"

"I don't trust anyone in law enforcement. My sister was working with the Feds. She was about to go into WitSec when Wren found her." She thanked Ash for the food. Despite losing her appetite at the mention of Wren's name, she managed to get a few bites down. "The best I can figure is there's some kind of leak in the government agency she worked with."

"Tell me everything you know about what happened to your sister." Ash leaned back, opened a drawer, and retrieved a laptop from the counter behind him.

Emery didn't realize she'd been holding her breath for the last few seconds until she blew out a deep sigh. "You didn't mention having a laptop before."

"It's for emergencies."

She clasped her hands together, placing them on the table. "Okay. Wren was bad news from the start. He was good looking and charming but slick. The kind of guy who knew all the right things to say because he'd practiced the lines so much on other people."

Ash nodded. His face pinched, like he didn't appreciate the idea of her thinking another man could be attractive.

"My first warning sign was the fact that he always used cash. He seemed to want to make sure Becca knew he had rolls of hundreds. Who carries around that kind of money other than my crazy aunt who used to hide it underneath her bed for safe keeping?"

"Kat and your aunt would've been great friends." He'd mentioned Kat several times. Stabs of jealousy took a shot at her.

"Is she crazy, too?"

The sound of tires on packed snow broke the conversation. Emery double timed it to the bathroom where she hid behind the cracked door. Panic that Wren had somehow tracked her down caused the air to thin.

Ash was to his feet and at the front window in a matter of seconds. "It's okay. It's her. She's most likely checking to make sure you're okay."

"How would she know I'm here?"

"She doesn't. But people around here check up

on each other. Sheriff called her place looking for me."

"Please don't let on that I'm here. The fewer people who know about me, the better. I don't want to risk—"

"Already on it." He hopped into his jeans and was out the front door almost as fast as he'd downed his first cup of coffee.

CHAPTER 6

"Morning, Kat." Ash ignored the frigid temperatures as he approached the widow's pickup. The window was rolled down. "What can I do for you?" This was a bad time to realize he wasn't wearing shoes.

"Stopped by to check on the car wreck." She eyed him up and down, a knowing twinkle in her eyes. Damn, she was suspicious. He didn't want to lie to someone who'd showed him such kindness and he considered Kat a dear friend, but Emery's wasn't his secret to share.

"Everything's fine." And it would be. That much was truth.

Ash really should've put on a shirt. Another wind gust blasted through him. Coming from the desert to this was definitely a shock to the system. Those few months of summer followed by fall here did nothing to prepare him for this kind of cold.

"As much as I'm enjoying the gun show," those eyes twinkled with mischief this time, "you should get back inside before you freeze to death. Or if you're happy to keep posing like that, you'd make a great statue for the inn. You'd probably attract a lot of womenfolk to stay; I could raise my rates." She laugh-snorted, clearly tickled with herself.

"I could always go in the backroom with the heat lamps to warm me up." He referenced the room she'd asked him not to go inside of, the pot room.

"Honey, you're already bringing enough heat. You'll melt the snow if you're not careful," she winked.

"I'll have to keep covered up then. We don't want the roads to ice." Their easy banter was one of the many reasons Ash had decided to stick around in Hero's Junction even though Texas called to him. Although, with Emery at his side, he might be able to face his home state again for more than a week.

"The driver is fine. Had a place to stay last night. Said something about the rental company sending a replacement as soon as the weather cleared."

"Storm hit pretty bad a couple miles north." Ash

would check the weather before he and Emery set out to…hell…he had no idea where she'd been heading. She hadn't exactly been forthcoming when he first met her. He was just now getting her to warm up enough to trust him.

"The road from here to the inn must be okay," he stated the obvious. She was here. The roads couldn't have been too bad—Kat wasn't one to drive if it wasn't safe.

She nodded. "We got off easy. The resorts got good powder. Should bring on the skiers and snowboarders over the next few days. Phone's been ringing and I'm getting bookings."

Ash shivered despite the good news. It was asscold outside. He'd never understand people who voluntarily strapped wood sticks to the bottom of their feet and rocketed down a snow-capped mountain. Though when he thought about the adrenaline rush he reconsidered. If the rush was anything like the rush he'd felt last night with Emery, maybe there was something to skiing after all. "I'll stop by in a few days to check on you."

She held up a cell phone. "It'd be a helluva lot easier if you'd just give in and take one of my spares."

He put his hands in the surrender position. "What would I do with one of those?"

"I don't know…take a call from a dear old lady."

"Not fair. I know you didn't just play the sympathy card." He laughed despite losing feeling in his fingers and toes.

"Get inside before you draw a crowd." Kat laughed at her own joke. She waved before putting the gearshift in reverse. She pursed her lips. "Alton said there was a man in town this morning asking if a woman had come through in the past twenty-four hours."

"What'd you tell him?"

"To mind his own business. Folks come through here all the time. Hero's Junction is on the way to one of the most popular ski resorts in Colorado. What the hell did he expect?"

ASH TOOK the porch in one leap and immediately moved to the fireplace. "She's gone. You can come out now."

A breeze blew through him, and the cold bit hard.

He scanned the room, realized the kitchen window was open about the same time he heard his truck engine roar to life.

Shit. Hell. Fuck.

Emery was in freeze, flight or fight mode. Good to know which instinct kicked in for her in the heat of the moment...flight.

"Stop." His shouts to the rear of his vehicle brought brake lights. At least she'd listened to him. He could work with that. He ate up the real estate between him and his truck with his arms in plain sight, like calming a wild animal.

"I'm sorry. I panicked." The emotions playing out on her features softened his frustration. "I thought he was here and I climbed out the window before I could stop myself."

"Do you want my help, because you're not making this easy." Yeah, he snapped. What the hell did she expect.

"I know. And it's obvious, even to me, that I do *need* help. But asking for it. Putting someone else's life at risk..." Those cinnamon eyes of her filled with water and her chin quivered. "I care about you more than I have anyone in a very long time...probably ever. The thought of anything happening to you because of me scares the hell out of me."

A gust of wind blasted right through him. "Turn off the engine and let's go back inside. We can come up with a plan together, but *we* will never be anything if you keep running every time you get scared. I've faced scarier men than Wren. I know how to survive. If you want justice for your sister, you need me."

His words must've scored a direct hit because she cut off the engine, followed him inside, and then handed over the keys.

He topped off his coffee mug. "You want another cup?"

"Yes." Her voice was small and he'd be damned if it didn't break down more of his walls. "I can get it myself, though."

If she kept it up he might feel rejected. "It's okay to let someone else help you."

"I know that."

"Do you, though?" He couldn't stop the disappointment from slipping out. He'd been around plenty of scared people before. Not everyone bolted at the first sign of trouble. If this relationship was going to have a fighting chance, she'd have to learn to trust him.

She plopped down in the chair at the table. "After losing our parents, I stepped into the role of mother, father and protector for Becca." Her chin jutted out as he handed over the full mug. "Relying on someone else is new for me. I'm not good at it. But I want to try."

Ash took a seat at the two-top. He could work with that. "Tell me about everything you know about Wren."

"He's a class-A jerk. I knew he was bad for my sister the minute I met him. I expected him to break her heart. I didn't realize he'd be dangerous. My miscalculation cost her everything—"

Emery studied the rim of her coffee cup like she needed a distraction, so she wouldn't lose it.

Ash couldn't stay mad at her. "How old was your sister?"

"Twenty-seven."

"What happened to her isn't your fault, Emery. Twenty-seven is old enough to make her own decisions." Damn those words, true as they were, because he'd been doing a similar thing. Blaming himself for living when his buddies were killed.

"I should've done more to make her see him for what he is." Emery looked away, losing the battle against tears.

"Did you warn her about Wren?"

"Yes. Multiple times."

"Did you explain why you thought he was bad for her?"

"Every chance I got. That's probably why she ran to him in the first place. She was trying to prove me wrong."

"Hold on. You do realize blaming yourself for the actions of another person isn't being fair to yourself." The irony in his words tasted bitter as hell. Isn't that what he'd been doing for the past eight months? Blaming himself for being the one to come back to the States alive?

Emery chewed on her bottom lip as she kept her gaze focused toward the window. She seemed to be considering his point. If he was going to give advice and mean it, he needed to consider forgiving himself.

"From what you've told me so far, Wren seems like a charmer. Most people don't see the insincerity when they get caught up with a man like him. His charms weren't turned on you. Made it easier to see him for the bastard manipulator he is."

Emery wiped her eyes. "You're so right. Talking to her, hearing her expound on his good qualities—qualities I sure as hell didn't see—made me feel like she'd joined a cult."

"I'm guessing she came around to visit less and less."

"Yes. Why do you say that?" Cinnamon eyes blinked at him. She stood and started pacing.

"The first thing a guy like him does is cut out family members."

"Wasn't hard to do in this case, considering I'm all she had. I was busy teaching. When the semester's in full swing my days are long. I'd been asked to cover for a sick colleague and was helping a T.A. get her bearings."

"Wren most likely took advantage of the timing. A guy like that'll use any advantage he can get. You're strong. There's no way he wanted a woman like you in her ear."

"I just wish my sister could've told me what he was doing that was illegal. She said the Feds were on the wrong track and gave me an address. Our conversation was interrupted and the next thing I know I'm burying her."

Ash tugged her toward him and she settled on his lap, sitting sidesaddle. He wrapped arms around her and held onto her. She turned her face toward him and kissed him. "I'm sorry about before. I don't want to keep running. You're worth sticking around for."

Those words cracked more of the casing around his heart. "Good. Because I'm falling for you, Emery."

She seemed to understand he didn't take those words lightly.

"There are other ways to check out an address without actually visiting a location." He grabbed his laptop.

"I started to use one of the computers at school. Didn't know if I was being watched or not. I certainly didn't want to use my laptop at home. A white minivan had been parked at the end of my block for a few days. It made me wonder."

"No one should be able to connect the two of us. I knew a guy who was good with computers. He scrambled my IP address."

"That's handy."

"You need to know there's a man in town asking if a woman had come through. Kat mentioned it when she stopped by." He could feel her muscles tense and steadied himself for when she tried to bolt.

"I...WE...SHOULD GO." Emery tried to slow her breathing but all she could hear was the sound of her racing heart.

"Hold on. He doesn't know anything about me and no one around here will tell him."

No one had had Emery's back in so long she almost couldn't fathom an entire community coming together to protect her. She might like to settle down in a place like Hero's Junction someday. Right now, she had to figure out what Becca was trying to tell her.

"Is it safe to be here?" How he figured out where she was headed was a good question.

"Leaving, getting on the road now could be riskier than staying put. It's light outside and Tabasco isn't exactly hard to miss."

"You named your truck Tabasco?"

"It seemed to fit."

"Staying here feels like doing nothing." The air in her lungs deflated.

"What if we run into him on the road?" Emery didn't get the sense that Ash doubted his own abilities for one second. He was used to working alone or with trained soldiers at his side. She had no training, no ability to handle a gun. All she had was survival instinct and a need for justice that ran so deep it carved lines through her heart.

"Keeping yourself alive is the best way to ensure justice for your sister. That's what you want, right? The end game is Wren behind bars for life so the bastard pays for his crimes."

Slowly, she nodded.

"He'll look for you in public places. Restaurants and inns are off limits for now. No one knows you're here. If Kat figured it out, and that is a possibility, she wouldn't tell him or anyone else." Ash's fingers danced across the keyboard.

His strong arms around her tethered her to reality.

"We'll figure this out." Ash kissed the nape of her neck. His warm breath and tender touch stirred her heart. And she wanted to believe him.

"You're willing to put yourself on the line for me?" She realized she'd said the words out loud.

"Yes." Another kiss and more of her resolve melted. Being determined not to give in to love—love?—might not be her best quality but she'd convinced herself somewhere down the line that it was how she'd survived on her own all these years. It was how she'd been strong for Becca.

Emery had set her own needs aside the day her parents died. It had started a few years before when her mother was diagnosed with Non-Hodgkins Lymphoma. Emery had approached her mother's illness the way most eighteen-year-olds did. She assumed her mother would live forever.

A new drug gave her mother life. She'd taken all

the medications like clockwork, even when they'd made her sick. During the darker days before she started recovering, Emery made a promise to her mother. No matter what happened, Emery would always take care of Becca. It wasn't a commitment she'd planned to need to follow through on, but she meant it just the same.

The medicine had worked. Her mother's health improved. And then almost a year later...the car crash.

Something inside Emery snapped the day she lost her parents. Her sole mission became following through on her promise to her mother, on taking care of Becca.

When the time had come to step back and let her baby sister fly on her own, Emery couldn't do it. She held on tighter when she should've trusted her sister and let her make mistakes while she was young.

Eventually, Becca had pushed her sister away.

Looking back, there was a moment when Emery saw the gap between them become a chasm. She'd panicked and thrown herself into work. It was easy to stay busy during the semester.

The distance between them grew. Wren swooped in like a bird of prey. Becca was in too deep before she realized what she'd gotten herself into.

"All I'm getting on the map from that address is an abandoned house on acreage. Doesn't look like anyone's been there for a while." Ash's voice drew her out of her heavy thoughts. "Does this ring any bells?"

"Not really." She repositioned on his lap, so she could see the screen. There was nothing that stood out about the one-story cabin, except the isolation and the fact that Becca had never mentioned this place before. Had Wren taken her sister there?

He moved the picture to street view. "Looks like it's for sale."

Emery picked up the pen and legal pad on the table next to the laptop. "Can you zoom in enough to find out who has the listing?"

"No." Getting that close only made the picture blurry. "I can do one better." He poked at the keys until a real estate site came up. He entered the address. "Shawn Joplin."

"Wait a minute. My sister mentioned that name before." She took down his number from the listing.

He pulled up the realtor's picture and blew it up.

"Do you recognize him?"

EMERY STUDIED THE PHOTO. She blew out a long sigh and Ash felt her chest deflate. "No. I want to call him but…"

"You're afraid to tip him off if he's in cahoots with Wren."

"He could be his partner in crime." Emery tapped her index finger on the notepad in her hand.

"Two options strike me. She's either warning you or giving you a lead to hand over to the Feds."

"She said they were on the wrong track. I doubt she wants me to hand over his name. She said she had proof of Wren's crimes."

"Sounds like the government was trying to force her to testify against him and she was afraid to give up what she really knew."

"My sister sounded very afraid on the phone call. She wasn't her usual self and hadn't been the last couple of times we'd talked. If I'd been paying better attention I would've picked up on it at the time. I thought she was being moody. She'd call and then cut me off by saying she had to go."

"Where does Wren live?"

"Fort Worth." Ash doubted the man would be expecting them to show at his home. What about his place of business? From the internet, he'd learned Wren was a real estate developer.

Ash pulled up Wren's address online. Next, he pulled up the location Becca had given Emery. There was no easy connection. "Realtors and real estate developers naturally work together. Those two having an association made perfect sense. Joplin could be a friend of Wren's."

"Calling Joplin is a risk we have to take." Emery leaned against his chest and he wrapped his arms around her.

"I don't have a phone and we can't go to Kat's." Ash looked up Joplin's office information on the internet. He plugged the address into the online map. "That's a forty-five-minute drive from here."

"There's a temporary phone in my purse. I picked it up at a convenience store off the highway in case of emergency." She pushed off his lap and retrieved it.

"Put it on speaker and you do the talking. Make an appointment. Tell him you'll be bringing your fiancé and the two of you are house hunting."

"What if he asks where I'm from?"

"Be as honest as you can be. Say your fiancé lives here. His place is too small for both of you."

"Why not ask him about Wren over the phone? Or if he knew my sister?"

"I'll be able to tell a lot about him face-to-face."

That made sense to her. A man with Ash's training had most likely needed interview skills.

They couldn't make progress without taking calculated risks.

"Here goes." Emery gave him a look before making the call.

CHAPTER 7

"Shawn Joplin, can I help you?" If the man was under duress he sure as hell didn't sound like it. Hearing his voice, knowing she was one step closer to getting justice for Becca caused her hands to tremble and her heart to hammer against her ribs.

"Hi, my name is," she glanced at the counter and somehow came up with, "Sarah. I'm moving to Colorado where my fiancé lives and we're looking for a bigger space. There's no way I'll fit all my stuff in his closet."

Joplin chuckled. "That's a common problem. Did you have an area in mind?"

"He probably does, since he knows Colorado better than I do. He gets off at," she glanced at Ash who held up three fingers, "three o'clock. Is that a good time for us both to come in and meet with you?"

"Hold on a sec, let me check my schedule. I can move this showing up, so yes. I can do three o'clock." Shawn had an upbeat quality to his voice. He sounded young. Based on the picture posted on the web, he was close in age with Becca. Ash guessed the man could be considered attractive by most standards. He looked like he could walk off a billboard for a men's clothing designer.

"Great." Emery seemed to be forcing a smile and her voice reflected cheeriness that didn't reach her eyes. "See you then."

"What's your fiancé's name?" Joplin asked.

"Tim Bur...g. That's spelled B-U-R-G." She glanced at Ash with a nervous look. It was pretty clear based on her tense expression she feared she'd just given them up.

He winked to give her some measure of reassurance. She was doing fine. Better than fine. She got the meeting setup and Joplin didn't seem the wiser.

"I look forward to meeting you and Mr. Burg at three o'clock." His voice had a chirpy, I'm-about-to-make-money quality. Mid-February during a snow storm meant slow business in Colorado real estate. The only folks making money were the ones selling condos at nearby resorts. Based on the scant number of this guy's listings on the web, his business was as dry as Texas soil in summer.

Between getting dressed, tending to Seven and eating a late lunch, Ash had them on the road by two o'clock. Seven sat on the bench seat in between them during the forty-five-minute drive. Emery surprised herself with how quickly she'd become comfortable with him. He'd been nothing but calm around her. There was comfort in his routine.

The sun tucked behind towering mountains, so it was already getting dark outside.

"Do you miss it?" Emery stroked Seven's fur. "Texas."

"I'd be lying if I said I didn't. I miss the wide-open spaces and a sky that seems to go on forever. I miss daylight, especially since the sun starts disappearing at around this time every day."

"Would you consider moving back?"

"For the right reason." Or person. He didn't say the words but the innuendo hung in between them. "What about you? You're a teacher. Do you like what you do?"

"I did at first. The whole reason I got into teaching was to make a difference in a child's life. Teenage years are tough but I actually like working with fifteen-year-olds. It's a critical age because they're starting to find new ways to define themselves. They push parents away and are looking for role models."

"What about now?"

"Honestly? There's too much paperwork, too much pressure to push a kid through because he's a star on the football field. Not enough freedom to be able to make the difference I want to make."

"Sounds about right." Ash figured not much had changed since he'd been in high school. All the attention went to athletes. He should know. He'd been one of them. He'd also been one of the few who cared about his report card and had a decent brain, which allowed him to get by without the help of tutors. "Are you considering leaving teaching?"

"After I finish the semester I might. I don't know what's been going on in my mind recently. Losing my sister…it's causing me to change in some ways."

"Kind of makes you rethink everything in your life when you lose someone close to you out of the blue, doesn't it?" His voice was so low it was practically a whisper but he could tell she'd heard him. He'd felt that sucker punch himself. knew all about the sucker punch that was.

"I understand why you ended up in Hero's Junction. Seems like a nice place to hang your hat for a while."

"It's been good to me. But it's not Texas. It's not home." The truck had been winding up, down and around for a solid forty-five minutes when the realtor's office came into view. It was on the left-hand-side of the road, literally positioned in between two hills. "Looks like we made it to Joplin's office."

"And right on time." Emery tapped the face of her watch.

There was a small parking lot and row of doors. A dentist, a title company and a realtor's office made up the entire suite. The building itself was made of brown brick. There was a covered concrete porch with white columns, and a railing in front like back in the old days when a horse needed to be tied up. The place was a throwback, it was nostalgia and Ash had to admit it worked. Thoughts of horseback riding, tumbleweeds and simpler days came to mind.

Four cars parked in a row off to one side of the building. There were two hand-carved wooden benches flanking the middle door which lead to the realtor's office of Mountainside Realty. A blanket was strewn across one of the benches and a yellow tabby curled on top of it.

Ash parked the truck.

"Ready?" Emery blew out a breath like she was shoring up her resolve.

"Let's do this."

Nose to the ground, Seven searched the perimeter of the building. Emery waited alongside Ash, thinking how trapped she'd become by her own habits, by her old way of thinking.

It was time for a change.

"Maybe you should walk in front to block me, in case he knows who I am."

Seven moved to the porch, ready to investigate inside the building.

"I was just about to suggest the same thing." He linked their hands, his right to her left. And then he surprised her with a tender kiss on the lips.

She thought it might be for show until he added, "We might have only known each other for hours instead of days but you're already special to me. I can't explain it or maybe I don't want to try. I care about you. This, what we have, could grow into something real. Not just for show, like the one we're about to put on."

"I'm counting on it." The feeling was very real.

Her past self never would've believed in love at first sight. Thinking she could have a future with a man she'd met twenty-four hours ago would've seemed absurd to her.

It had happened for her parents and they'd celebrated twenty-two years of marriage before the accident. They'd been in love. She'd witnessed it firsthand.

Ash gave her another sweet kiss before tucking her behind him and making his way toward the door. She loved the feel of his rough hand against hers.

Seven stood at attention at the door. He seemed to have no interest in the yellow tabby and the cat was just about as enthused, rolling onto her side and cleaning the fur on her stomach. It was the equivalent of a human yawn.

A receptionist smiled the minute the door opened and they walked in. The chime seemed overkill considering they couldn't exactly sneak in with her desk five feet away and her chair aimed at the front door.

Seven went right to work, moving swiftly around the room.

"He's a war hero," Emery said with a surprising amount of pride.

"Then we should let him work." The blond-haired, blue-eyed woman stood. "You must be the couple Shawn is expecting. I'm Lucinda. I'll let him know you're here."

"Thank you." Ash's gaze swept the room, a stark reminder of just how dangerous this could be.

Emery slipped behind him. It wasn't difficult to disappear behind his tall, muscled frame.

A man who matched the image of Shawn Joplin from the internet emerged from the hallway wearing a crisp buttoned-up white shirt and a wide smile. "Tim Bur—"

Shawn froze. His face dropped. She half expected him to bolt out the back door but instead he turned sheet-white.

The receptionist popped out from behind him, looking confused. He glanced at her, gave a quick smile, and turned to Ash. "Mind if we meet in my office?"

"After you." Ash held tight to her fingers, the link kept her heart from racing out of control.

The hallway had two doors. Seven finished his work and joined them in Shawn's office, the second door. Inside, there were two orange metal and plastic chairs across from his desk and a small swivel chair. There was a painting on the wall of a sunset.

The signature of the artist on the bottom right of the picture said whoever painted it was a relative of Shawn's. A wife?

Emery glanced at his wedding finger. No band. She also noticed there weren't any pictures around of him with a wife or kids.

"Something awful must've happened for you to be here." He looked directly at Emery as he took a seat and then twisted his hands together on top of the desk. Sadness overtook his light blue eyes. He had that Ken-doll look, if there'd been a snowboarder version of the doll.

"You know who I am?"

He nodded. "Becca talked about you all the time in college. She'd show me pictures of the two of you. You haven't changed or aged."

His face lit up when he talked about Becca. Emery's heart squeezed. The thought of never seeing her sister again had to be pushed aside or it would have the power to break Emery. She needed to be strong for her sister.

"You're from Texas?" Talking to someone who seemed to know her sister so well that Emery had never met or heard of struck another chord. There was so much Becca kept to herself, so much of her life she didn't share even in college.

"Born and bred in Abilene. Came to Fort Worth for school. Becca and I met while working at the Burger Joint." His shoulders slumped and she could guess what his next question would be. "Did something happen to her?"

Emery couldn't say the words. She couldn't look into his hopeful blue eyes and deliver the kind of blow that would come next, the one she hadn't had time to process herself.

"Becca is gone." Ash's low and respectful voice gave her such a sensation of reverence.

"Oh. God. No." Shawn balled his fist and slammed it against the desk.

A few rogue tears slipped out. Emery wiped them away as discreetly as she could manage. Let those flood gates open and there'd be no stopping it. This was the first real friend of Becca's Emery had met. Sitting and crying in his office when there was a possibility she could get critical information from him would take time she didn't have to waste.

"What happened?" Shawn looked to be struggling to maintain composure.

"We have reason to believe she was murdered." Emery barely got the words out.

Shawn pinched his lips together like he didn't want to say the next words. "I can't believe she's...

gone. She hasn't been posting on social but that was Becca. Always living in the moment. She'd get too busy to update her page. And ever since I moved out here we've talked less and less."

"How long have you been here?" Emery wondered if the timeline matched up with Becca dating Wren.

"Since about this time last year." Emery had no idea that her sister had a friend who'd moved to Colorado. That's how little Becca shared.

Something else dawned on her. "You don't seem surprised that I had no idea who you are. I mean, you and my sister must've been pretty close and she never mentioned you to me."

"Becca liked to keep her life compartmentalized. I asked to meet you way back in college. It wasn't like I was trying to hide the fact that Becca and I were close. She said she wanted to keep our friendship separate. Whatever that meant. We used to be two peas in a pod until this past year. You know how it goes. New city. Our relationship hit the occasional 'like' on social media level. Until last month. She called me and we caught up with each other. She said she wanted to come for a visit and not to be surprised if she just showed up out of nowhere."

She glanced at Ash, who had become her lifeline.

Doing any of this without him would be impossible. A very real part, very deep-seated part of her needed his strength, his determination. She didn't want to consider what kind of life she'd be going back to when she left Colorado.

"When Becca got back in touch with me she said she needed a favor and that I could refuse if I wanted to," remorse darkened his light eyes. "I should've known something was up." Shawn balled his fists again. "I should've forced her to tell me what she was up to."

Emery had been living that hell—the hell of wishing she could go back and change the past. She almost couldn't believe she was about to say this considering the hell she'd put herself through over it. "None of this is your fault, Shawn. It sounds like you were a good friend to my sister and she needed that. She could've gone to you for help. Heaven knows I was there for her. This didn't have to happen to her."

Those last words stung. The truth had a way of doing that—of hitting her right in the solar plexus.

CHAPTER 8

"SHE TOLD me to tell you something but for the life of me I can't remember what she said." Shawn twisted his hands together.

Frustration wouldn't help Shawn remember. If it would, Emery could go all-in. Being this close to answers with the thought of going home empty-handed made her sick. Home? She couldn't go there until Wren was locked up behind bars where he belonged.

After spending the past twenty-four hours with Ash, McKinney didn't feel so much like home. He felt like home now. A house without him was just brick and mortar.

Emery thought back to the last phone call she'd had with her sister and the first clue Becca might be in trouble. Her sister mentioned witness protection but that the Feds had the evidence all wrong. Wren would get off scot-free and she would be in hiding for the rest of her life, living in fear.

Before her sister could say anything else, she'd said, "Oh, hello, Wren. I wasn't expecting you home this early."

A male voice mumbled something in the background that Emery couldn't pick up. The few times she'd met him she didn't care for how quietly he spoke. Not because he was a gentle spirit. Because he wanted everyone to have to lean in to hear him.

"I'm talking to my friend, Pam," she'd said. And then Becca returned to the line. "I have to go. I was only calling to tell you that Mary's mother died and I need to run by the family's house and drop off some flowers. If you stop by will you send my condolences?"

The few times Becca and Emery had spoken on the phone recently her sister had lied about who she was talking to. That didn't sound any big alarms at first. One comment did. Mary's mother died ten years ago.

The family had lived in Colorado at 224 Wickland Street.

"The first few steps of this plan were well

thought out." Ash's voice broke through her heavy thoughts.

Emery couldn't agree more. "She must've seen this coming for a while."

"Leads me to believe she was orchestrating a plan and the reason it seems haphazard here at the end is because she thought she had more time." Ash leaned forward and rested his elbows on his knees.

She turned her attention to Shawn. "Do you recall any of the conversation you had with my sister? Maybe starting at the beginning will jar your memory."

"We talked about the possibility of her moving to Colorado next year before she got mixed up with her new boyfriend," he glanced from Emery to Ash, "I'm guessing that's the Wren you two have been talking about."

Emery nodded.

"Once he came into the picture we didn't talk as much. I always thought that was odd because boyfriends never got in the way of our friendship in the past. This guy became her whole world in a hot minute. I didn't push the issue, either. I had enough on my plate with the move and I guess I figured she'd come to her senses and leave him."

"She might have been trying." Emery's point seemed well-taken when Shawn nodded. "Can you back up to the very last time you spoke?"

"I wish I could remember. Don't get me wrong, I love Becca. I can't even begin to imagine her…" He paused a couple of beats like the storm of emotion would pass if he gave it a minute. He cracked a half-smile when he continued. "She was dramatic. I thought she was being over-the-top. If I'd known, I would've taken her words seriously."

"Believe me, I would've ignored less and acted on my instincts more, too," Emery said softly.

"I do remember that it was something off-the-cuff sounding. Something like, 'if anything happens to me it's really important to tell my sister to remember…. Didn't make a bit of sense to me when she said it." He smacked the desk with the flat of his palm. His eyes lit up. "Pandora's Box."

"I know exactly what that means." Emery pushed to standing before he could ask another question. "Don't take what I'm about to say the wrong way because it's easy to see how much you loved my sister. The little you know, the better."

Ash was already on his feet, his hand on her elbow. Seven took point.

"Thank you for your time, Shawn." She hated to leave like this but if she'd made the connection to Shawn based on the address her sister had given for the fake funeral Wren could, too.

"How busy has it been at work, lately?" Ash asked Shawn.

"It's been a ghost town."

"There a place you can go for a few days where you can stay under the radar?" Ash must've been thinking the same thing she was. Involving Shawn put him at risk.

It made even more sense to Emery now when she thought about how Becca had lied to Wren about their conversations. At the time, Emery had the impression her sister was ashamed to admit the two were talking. Even though phone chats might've been few and far between Emery had always carved out time for her baby sister.

The fact that Becca had strung together clues only Emery could piece together touched her. Her sister realized that Emery would stop at nothing to bring justice to the man who'd taken her life far too young.

Becca had paid the ultimate price for her secrets, for not knowing when to ask for help.

"She was trying to take him down on her own,"

she said to Ash as soon as the three of them were inside the truck, the door closed.

He put the gearshift in reverse and backed out of the parking spot. "What does Pandora's Box mean?"

"It's at a lake house we used to go to in summer. There was a fireplace cleaning box that looked like it had never been used in the old house where we used to vacation with our parents. I think the place might have belonged to a relative on my Dad's side, maybe my great uncle. He lived to ninety-five." At ninety-five he lived a full life. Twenty-seven was too young to die.

Ash gripped the steering wheel and clenched his jaw.

It struck Emery how much he'd lost. "I'm sorry. Talking about all this death when you lost people who were like family must not be easy."

"Ignoring it hasn't made the pain any better, either. Guess it's time to face it head-on." He reached over Seven and touched her hand. "Keep talking."

"Best as I can remember the family sold the place after he passed, so we stopped vacationing there. When we were kids, we used to leave 'secret' messages for each other in the box because we could access it when we were outside. It came in handy when my sister got in trouble and had to stay in to think about her actions."

"Becca sounds like she had a big personality." The hint of admiration in his tone warmed her.

"That's an understatement." Becca would've like Ash. "We were supposed to be separated and I hated that she was stuck inside when it was a gorgeous day. So, I'd slip notes to her through the box. Naming it Pandora's Box kept our parents clueless. We could talk about it with them in the same room at dinner and they didn't know what we were up to."

"Sounds like you had a few cards up your sleeve." Emery used to be playful. She used to have more fun. Life got a little too real, a little too serious after her parents died. She'd stepped up and into a parenting role when she was barely an adult herself. She'd made mistakes. Maybe every parent did. Maybe it was time to forgive herself for hers.

"There was a boy my sister had a crush on. Matt Carson. I ended up the go between, delivering his messages to her."

"What's the address of the lake house?"

She rattled it off from memory. There was no way she could forget a place that held so many warm memories of her family. "It's near Fort Worth. Do you know the area?"

"No. Figure we can look it up on the map back at the cabin." He navigated onto the winding road.

From the rearview, she could see that Shawn had taken their warning seriously. He was in the driver's seat of his Jeep, turning west, the exact opposite direction she and Ash were heading in.

Ash punched the gas pedal harder. "I'll need to make a pitstop for a few road trip supplies and call in a favor."

"THANKS FOR THE LIFT, JOE." Joseph 'Kujo' Kuntz had dark hair and dark stubble on his chin. He'd responded to Ash's outreach within minutes by offering to pick them up in a friend's chopper.

"Call any time you need a hand. It's good seeing you both." Joe had been patient when Seven needed to inspect the chopper before anyone could get inside. His experience showed in the way he interacted with Seven, calm and authoritative. "You're doing a great job with him, by the way."

Ash doubted it. "We'll get there someday."

"It's not easy but it's worth it." Joe saluted and climbed back inside the chopper.

"I owe you big time. For Seven, and now this."

Joe smiled and tossed a set of keys to Ash. "You did me a favor with Seven. I'd say we're even now. A friend dropped off a vehicle for you to use while you're in town."

Ash wouldn't look a gift horse in the mouth. "Thank you. For everything."

With a salute and a smile, Joe was back in the sky.

Ash checked out the private airport parking lot. Nose to ground, Seven went ahead, searching for explosives he wouldn't find.

"Did he say which one?" Emery pointed toward the half dozen vehicles parked in the lot.

Ash clicked the door lock on the key fob and got a reaction from a black SUV. "That one right there."

The lake house was a twenty-minute drive from the private airport. Ash made it in sixteen.

The house itself looked to have been built in the late fifties. Ash had grown up in a neighborhood that had been built around the same time, so he recognized the construction.

"The fireplace was on the side of the house." Emery blew out a breath. "I just hope we're on the right track."

"You call anything else Pandora's Box?"

She was already shaking her head before he finished the question.

"There's only one way to find out." The first issue was finding evidence, if there was any. The bigger problem would come with trying to figure out what to do with it, once they had it in their hands. Law enforcement needed to be involved. That much was obvious.

Ash skimmed the house for signs of anyone being home. There was no car parked in the porte-cochere.

"I can knock. You'll get a minute to check the cleaning box while I distract anyone who might be home."

"*If* they come to the door. Some people don't answer if they're not expecting anyone." She made a good point.

"We'll hope knocking will be enough noise to cover for you. Seven will want to check the property. Take him with you. That way, people will think he ran off and you're corralling him."

She nodded. Tension lines bracketed her pink lips. Ash could only imagine what must be going through her thoughts right now. The hope at being so close to finding the evidence she needed to make sure the bastard who'd murdered her sister paid for what he'd done. He couldn't go there with the possibility this was a misstep and Pandora's Box meant something altogether different.

After clearing the porch steps in a couple of strides Ash peeked inside. The ornate door was half glass. Sheets covered furniture in the living room. Whoever owned this place didn't use it full-time. Becca must've realized the owner of a lake house in Texas wouldn't have much need for it in February. Places like this were summer residences and most used only on weekends.

Even so, there was no need to stick around once she collected the evidence.

"I got something." Emery rounded the side of the house, holding a flash drive in the palm of her hand.

Seven froze. His hackles raised. It was probably an animal. Ash had no plans to stick around long enough find out. His right hand spasmed. The keys hit the ground with a jingle. He retrieved them with his left. Retraining himself to be a leftie was a work-in-progress to say the least. "Let's get out of here."

The longer they were out in the open, exposed, the more difficult it would be for him to ensure her safety. He called Seven to the SUV.

"Where to?" Emery snapped her seatbelt into place and then held up the flash drive.

"We need to get out of here. Wren could be anywhere." Ash backed out of the drive.

"You don't think he's still in Colorado?"

"No one saw you there aside from myself and Shawn. The rental car you used will trace back to your neighbor. Until we know what's on that flash drive we don't know what we're dealing with. Best not to take anything for granted."

"We're in his territory now, aren't we?"

Ash nodded, focusing on the patch of road in front of him. Weeds slapped at the SUV as he drove down the narrow gravel roadway and back onto the main road.

"I have a computer at my house." She studied the device in her hand.

"It'd be safer at an internet café. We'll find a motel room, somewhere we can pay cash that's not too picky about dogs. Something closer to the city."

Finding a place to fit the bill wasn't difficult. The motel was in plain view of the highway except for the parking lot, which was stashed behind a wood fence. He navigated off the highway and pulled around the side of the fence. There were a couple of trucks parked in the lot and not much else around.

"I can't account for what we'll find inside the room." He shot Emery an apologetic look. "Highway access might come in handy if we need to make a quick exit."

"All I care about is finding out what's on this drive." She held it up and Ash could see that her hand trembled. "This damn thing cost my sister's life."

CHAPTER 9

THE MOTEL HAD plenty of vacancies. Inside the room wasn't as bad as Emery feared. There was a king-sized bed, a nightstand and a chair tucked in the corner next to a reading lamp. The color scheme might still be stuck in the eighties, all pastels and seascape prints in silver frames, but the comforter looked surprisingly in good shape. All things considered, not bad for a place that could also be rented by the hour.

The flash drive was burning a hole in her pocket. The saying came from her dad and he'd said it literally dozens of times when she was little, had a couple of dollars to spend and begged to be taken to the candy store.

"Is it too soon to go to the Internet café?" Ash had

placed a cup of water on the floor for Seven, who'd made quick work emptying it.

"We should be okay. You'll have to go inside alone." He glanced toward Seven. "Most places won't allow him."

She hadn't thought of that. Seven had become as much family to her as Ash.

Within minutes they were back in the SUV. Emery tried to keep her nerves at bay. She held the flash drive tight in her fist, praying the contents could bring justice to Wren.

Thankfully, The Net wasn't far.

Ash pulled in front of the internet café and parked where he could easily watch the door. The entire store front was made from glass. The problem was the dark tint meant to block the sun from glaring on the monitors inside.

"Here goes," she said but he stopped her with a hand on her elbow. His right had tremors sometimes and she noticed them right then. The nerve damage had taken away his ability to rely on his right hand. The fact that he was training himself to use his left impressed her even more.

"Use my credit card." He reached for his wallet and produced a card. "Word might've gotten out that I took off. Wren could put two-and-two together and realize I'm with you. Mine's still safer than using yours."

She thanked him and took the plastic offering.

The cell in her purse buzzed. Emery answered on the second ring.

"It's Shawn." His familiar voice came across the line.

"Hey," she paused a beat, "are you okay?"

"Me, yeah. I'm calling to let you know my receptionist called to let me know there was a man at the office a few hours ago asking if she'd seen a woman who matched your description."

"What did she say?"

"She told him the truth. The only people who'd come through were an engaged couple who went by the last name Burg. Problem was he had a photo. It was you, Emery. And he flashed a badge."

"Did you ask what he looked like?"

"Five-feet-nine-inches give or take. Muscular build. Red hair, blue eyes. He introduced himself as Marshal Kevin Banks."

Emery relayed the information to Ash.

"She did the right thing, Shawn." Emery didn't want anyone lying to law enforcement on her behalf. "What about you? Did the marshal ask where you were?"

"Lucinda doesn't know, so that was easy. Do you have any idea what Becca might've gotten herself into?"

"We think we're close to figuring out. Stay out of sight until Ash calls. Okay?"

"Tell him to get rid of his phone. Don't keep it with him," Ash warned.

She did, realizing the feds would be able to track Shawn using his cell. The call rattled already tense nerves. Without another word, she slipped out of the SUV and into the sunlight.

Inside, she checked in with the attendant, nametag Dill. He led her straight to a computer and set her up. At three o'clock in the afternoon, she was the only person in the room besides him.

As soon as he walked away from the screen, Emery popped in the flash drive. A file folder popped onto the screen with a file name, that matched her own. Emery.

Emery clicked on the file. There were others once she drilled down. One was named, Pics. Another was marked, Video. The third was marked, Documents. Emery opened the first file.

Jesus.

It looked like the picture was taken from behind slats in a closet. There were more than a dozen images. Wren squeezed a wire around a man's neck. Emery recognized the man. He was a Fort Worth real estate developer, named T.J. Turner. T.J.'s disappearance had made headlines because his wife was believed to have been involved. Reports in the news had depicted her as a cheater. Foul play had been suspected. Without a body, no case could be made.

Emery felt sick looking at a picture of a man in his last seconds of life. Had Becca witnessed the murder?

Her sister must've felt alone and scared. The documents in the other file detailed out T.J.'s refusal to broker a sale of an old strip mall to Wren. Paperwork dated after T.J.'s death showed that a sale had gone through.

Emery wasn't sure she could stomach watching the video. She took in a fortifying breath and clicked. Becca's face filled the screen. She was in Wren's kitchen. It was dark inside the house, so she must've sneaked down to film in the middle of the night while he slept.

The sound was off. Emery located a pair of earbuds in her handbag and plugged them into the speaker. She restarted the video, fighting the sobs threatening to suck her under.

I'm so sorry for everything, Em. You have always been

an amazing big sister. You have always had my back and I don't think I told you nearly enough how much I love you.

Please make sure the evidence is turned in to the District Attorney. Don't trust anyone else.

I love you.

ASH NOTICED a sedan creep across the parking lot and park behind the building. He swept the area with his gaze. Emery was inside the building and he had no way to get word to her without leaving his vehicle. The other issue was that the vehicle had disappeared around the back. The folks inside could enter The Net from the rear and force her out the back door.

He palmed his weapon in his right hand. As much as he was trying to train with his left hand, his accuracy was nowhere near the right's.

"Let's move out." Seven followed Ash, nose to knee.

As soon as he slipped inside the door, a young guy popped from behind the counter at the back of the room waving his arms.

"Sorry, dude, no pets. Store policy."

"We're leaving." He looked at Emery, whose face had paled. He didn't want to acknowledge how much the thought of losing her gutted him.

She punched a few keys on the keyboard before pulling out the flash drive. "I'm done here anyway."

Seven spun around, started growling. He'd been trained to the scent of adrenaline. Trouble was coming.

"Out the back." Ash urged Emery toward the exit.

"What's going on here, dude?" The worker seemed to be catching on. He must not have seen the gun tucked behind Ash's leg.

"Get behind that counter, climb into a cabinet and hide. Some very bad men are coming through that door in a few seconds. They don't want you. Hide until the cops show up." Before Ash finished giving the order, the clerk disappeared behind the counter.

"Seven, come." The dog dutifully obeyed but was agitated over not being able to clear the place.

As the front door opened, Ash navigated them out the emergency exit. An alarm sounded, as the red sticker on the bar had promised. Good. He wanted law enforcement involved.

Weapon at the ready and with Emery tucked behind his back, he rounded the building. He needed to get them back to the SUV. Seven growled.

The glint of metal coming from the vehicle parked next to the SUV caught Ash's attention. A pair of men burst from the back of the building.

To their right was a ten-foot brick wall, blocking the strip mall from a neighborhood. Gun in front of them. Men with guns behind them. Cornered.

Seven, sensing the threat, went for the men.

Both had on jeans, sweatshirts and ball caps. One was tall, the other stocky. Tall took a step forward, aimed his weapon at Seven.

Ash had one chance to get this right. He took aim, squeezed the trigger.

The crack of a bullet pierced the air. A piece of Tall's hoodie flew off his right arm along with a smattering of blood. He dropped to his knees and grabbed at his bicep. His weapon tumbled to the ground, discharged. Thankfully, the bullet went astray. But Stocky took aim next. Tucking Emery behind him, Ash fired a second round with a shaky right hand. Missed. *Hell.*

The career sniper in him cringed at the fact he'd missed at this close range. He fired another round, aiming and hitting his mark in the hand.

Sirens could be heard in the distance. Help wouldn't get there in enough time.

Tall was already scrambling around for his weapon. Stocky was momentarily stunned but he'd regroup.

"Let's go." Ash pushed past those men and managed to get Emery back inside the store as another round tagged a brick next to his head.

Seven's nose was to the floor, checking the room, as Emery helped block the doorway. "Dill, where are the keys?"

Dill said something unintelligible.

"I need keys. *Now.*" Shouting would break through the kid's shock and spur him to action. It worked.

He tossed a set toward Ash as a round fired at the back door.

"Get down and underneath a desk," he instructed Emery.

Ash made a beeline for the front door. It opened. The man who she'd described as Wren stepped inside with his gun aimed at Ash's chest.

He dropped and rolled as a round pinged off the desk next to him. Wren was a better shot than Tall and Stocky. They were presently trying to kick down the back door.

"I know she's in here. Where are you, Emery?" Wren's voice was fingernails on a chalkboard.

On his belly, Ash crawled toward the sound of the man's voice. All he needed was one clear shot to take him down. Ash wouldn't shoot to kill. A man like Wren deserved to spend his life behind bars. Dying would be the easy way out.

Wren's tall frame came into view. It was then Ash realized he'd been nicked with a bullet in the thigh. He wasn't going to die but he was leaving a blood trail.

Ash leveled his gun at Wren, waiting for the shot. So much about being a great sniper involved patience.

Hackles raised, Seven growled at the threat.

"You stupid animal—"

In one swift motion, Emery shot out from behind a desk and tackled Wren before he could fire at Seven.

A crack split the air and time froze as Ash bolted toward the tangle of arms and legs. There was blood. Ash couldn't discern whose. He reared back his fist and slammed it into Wren's cheek, knocking the man unconscious.

With powerful thighs, he squeezed Wren's arms to his sides in case the man woke.

"Are you hit?" If anything happened to Emery…

There was blood on her shirt. She checked herself and paled when she caught sight of the amount of red.

"I don't think so."

Tires screeched in the parking lot. The cavalry had arrived.

Emery pushed to her feet and checked herself. "I'm not hit. I'm okay."

"Come out with your hands where we can see them." A loud voice boomed through a speaker.

"Go outside. Do as they say. Tell them what's going on in here. I'm not leaving this guy in here alone. Take Dill with you," Ash instructed. "Tell them about Seven. I don't want anyone coming in here and being surprised."

Emery coaxed Dill out from underneath the counter, put her hands on top of her head and then lead the way out the front door.

What felt like an eternity passed but it was most likely less than five minutes. Wren hadn't so much had an involuntary muscle twitch. Good. The bastard deserved everything he had coming to him and then some.

The glass door swung open.

"Put your hands where I can see 'em, sir." The

officer's voice was loud and agitated, his weapon directed at Ash.

Hands up, palms out Ash slowly raised to standing. He dug one foot into Wren's back. "My name is Ash Cage and the killer you're looking for in the Becca Freemont case is unconscious on the floor beneath me. He took a solid hit but I can't promise he won't wake up." He'd already kicked the weapons out of reach.

A second officer with his gun locked onto Ash entered the room. Both squatted, moving behind desks, obviously putting as much mass between them and danger as possible. "Hands on your head."

Seven growled.

"Heel, boy." Ash locked his fingers and rested them on the crown of his head. He hoped like hell he wouldn't pass out from blood loss. While he was wishing, he might as well go for it. He also prayed neither beat cop was trigger happy.

"Step toward us." The first officer barked the command. "And handle your dog."

"Yes, sir." Ash understood their need for safety, walking into a hot zone. "Seven, sit."

Seven did.

One of the officers holstered his weapon and closed the distance between him and Ash. After patting Ash down, he said into his radio, "He's clear."

Thankfully, Seven was used to being in high tension situations.

"Send him out," came the response. Ash figured he was about to meet the supervising officer running the show. He needed to warn the officers first. "The guy face down on the floor is dangerous. I kicked weapons out of his reach. He's unconscious for now. I knocked him out pretty good. Get there before he wakes and finds a gun. He won't hesitate to shoot."

The officer gave a nod of appreciation.

Outside, the sun was bright in the sky. Ash scanned faces, only one mattered to him right now. Emery. Relief washed over him when he saw her running toward him out of the corner of his eye.

"It's over, Ash." Her voice washed over him and through him.

Tears streaked her cheeks as she flew into his arms.

"It's over," he parroted.

He wasn't sure how long they stayed like that, in each other's arms. Five minutes? Ten? Long enough for a half-conscious Wren to be dragged out of the building in handcuffs and thrown into the back of a squad car.

Both Ash and Emery gave statements to the supervising officer, who thanked them for their courage and arranged for a water bowl to be brought to Seven. The District Attorney sent a courier to pick up the evidence. Dill was shaken but would be okay.

In the minutes that followed, the parking lot cleared out one-by-one. The Net closed for the rest of the day. All that was left to do was drive off and go back to their lives. Ash in Colorado and Emery in Texas. Two separate lives. Except Ash couldn't.

He took Emery's hands in his, bent down and took a knee. "Life is full of crazy twists and turns. And, yes, pain. I've lost enough to realize the people you care about can be gone in an instant. Not one of us is guaranteed to wake up tomorrow. Which means we should make the most of the time we have. I don't want to waste time, Emery. I'm in love with you. I want to spend whatever time we have together as husband and wife. Will you do me the incredible honor of marrying me?"

"I don't need more time to know how I feel about you, Ash. I love you. It hit me that first night we met. I'd never experienced anything like it before. I want to marry you. I want to be your family. I want to spend my life loving you." She kissed him. "I hope we have a long life together. But I'll take whatever time I can get."

Yes. That one word had the power to change everything. Ash was ready to live again. He was ready to move forward and let the past go.

But most importantly, he was ready to give his heart to the only woman he could ever love. He'd found home. Emery. *His* home.

KACE (Police and Fire: Operation Alpha)

A serial killer comes calling… After the devastating loss of his best friend in Kandahar, Kace Fox returns to his small Texas hometown, sells off his belongings and prepares to move as far away from anything and everything familiar as he can…Alaska. Hours before his flight, he learns the woman he had a fling with a few months ago—and can't get out of his thoughts—is missing. The small town of Blushing has a dark and dangerous secret. One that tried to kill Bree Burke and will come for her again. Kace puts his out-of-state move temporarily on hold to ensure Bree's safety while law enforcement searches for the killer dubbed, Gingerbread Man. When Kace learns the baby Bree is carrying very much belongs to him, he'll put everything on the line to save mother and child. To learn more, click here.

ABOUT BARB HAN

USA Today, Publisher's Weekly and Amazon Best-selling Author Barb Han lives in Texas—her true north—with her adventurous family, a spunky golden retriever-poodle mix, and too many books (if there is such a thing). She loves romance novels, thriller movies, and cooking. Her other hobbies include hiking, swimming, and skiing. Learn more about her books at www.BarbHan.com

ORIGINAL BROTHERHOOD PROTECTORS
SERIES

BY ELLE JAMES

Brotherhood Protectors Series

Montana SEAL (#1)

Bride Protector SEAL (#2)

Montana D-Force (#3)

Cowboy D-Force (#4)

Montana Ranger (#5)

Montana Dog Soldier (#6)

Montana SEAL Daddy (#7)

Montana Ranger's Wedding Vow (#8)

Montana SEAL Undercover Daddy (#9)

Cape Cod SEAL Rescue (#10)

Montana SEAL Friendly Fire (#11)

Montana SEAL's Bride (#12)

Montana Rescue

Hot SEAL, Salty Dog

ABOUT ELLE JAMES

ELLE JAMES also writing as MYLA JACKSON is a *New York Times* and *USA Today* Bestselling author of books including cowboys, intrigues and paranormal adventures that keep her readers on the edges of their seats. With over eighty works in a variety of sub-genres and lengths she has published with Harlequin, Samhain, Ellora's Cave, Kensington, Cleis Press, and Avon. When she's not at her computer, she's traveling, snow skiing, boating, or riding her ATV, dreaming up new stories. Learn more about Elle James at www.ellejames.com

Website | Facebook | Twitter | GoodReads | Newsletter | BookBub | Amazon

Follow Elle!
www.ellejames.com
ellejames@ellejames.com

Printed in Great Britain
by Amazon